MONTANA RANCH HIDEOUT

JULIE ARNOLD

Recycling programs for this product may not exist in your area.

ISBN-13: 978-1-335-91909-0

Montana Ranch Hideout

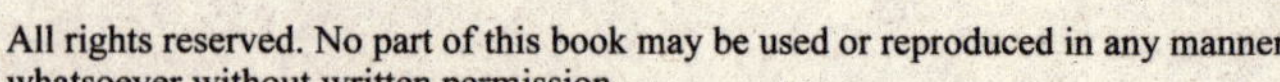

For questions and comments about the quality of this book, please contact us at CustomerService@Harlequin.com.

Love Inspired
22 Adelaide St. West, 41st Floor
Toronto, Ontario M5H 4E3, Canada
www.LoveInspired.com

HarperCollins Publishers
Macken House, 39/40 Mayor Street Upper,
Dublin 1, D01 C9W8, Ireland
www.HarperCollins.com

Printed in Lithuania

1 2 3 4 5 6 7 8 9 10 LIT 28 27 26 25

No way Ruby had fired those shots. No, someone was shooting *at* her, and she was running for her life.

Protectiveness streaked through Dex's veins as he spun his gray quarter horse, Moody, in a hairpin turn toward her.

"Dex!" Ruby's voice carried over the narrowing space separating them, pleading. Icy needles of fear stabbed at him, taunting him that he wouldn't reach her in time. That a bullet would blast through her and she would slip to the ground, lifeless.

"Hang on!" he yelled back, his voice rough as gravel. He would have flown to the rescue of any of his employees if they'd been in danger. But the fact that this was *Ruby* launched him into orbit.

Another crack exploded in the distance, flooding Dex's body with terror and rage. "Head down!" he shouted, but Ruby was already on it, plastering her small frame to her chestnut colt, Skinny, ducking her head of thick ebony hair behind the horse's broad neck.

She was less than a hundred feet away now, and Dex's mind raced through possible actions. His Winchester was strapped to his back, but he couldn't risk firing with Ruby this close. He needed to put her at a safe distance before targeting the threat...

Julie Arnold is a French speaker, slow runner and coffee lover who cannot help but make up stories. She grew up in Michigan but currently resides in Northwest Ohio with her husband and three children. The Lord has blessed her with a love for storytelling, so when she's not writing a book, she's probably curled up on the couch reading one.

Books by Julie Arnold

Love Inspired Suspense

Montana Ranch Hideout

Visit the Author Profile page at LoveInspired.com.

When I fall, I shall arise; when I sit in darkness,
the Lord shall be a light unto me.
—*Micah* 7:8

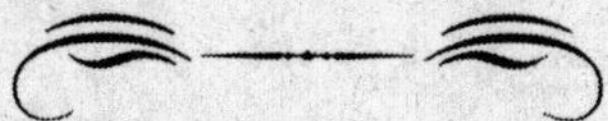

To Daniel, who always told me I could

ONE

Leaves rustled in the trees lining the horse trail and Ruby snapped her head up to scan the foliage. There wasn't a soul for miles on this lonely patch of ranch in Western Montana, and not the slightest breeze disturbed the sweltering, sun-baked landscape.

Ruby may be a city girl, new to ranch life, but she was fairly certain leaves didn't rustle on their own.

Her heart rate jumped, pelting her chest painfully, but she breathed through the sensation. It was probably a bird or a squirrel scampering along the branches. Ruby leaned into the warm, comforting presence of her chestnut colt, Skinny, seeking to calm her raw nerves. For the past four months in the Witness Protection Program, the peace of the fresh mountain air and the physical work on the ranch helped calm her restless heart and occupy her racing mind. She hadn't sensed the slightest danger since arriving at Dexler Acres, and she'd nearly convinced herself she was safe.

But "nearly" wasn't good enough for her ginned-up reflexes, always on high alert since the murder of her mother. Since she'd assumed the identity of Ruby Laurier, ranch hand, to evade her mother's killer until she could testify against him.

You are Ruby, even in the silence of your thoughts. You

are no longer Isadora de la Cruz, FBI agent, and you cannot slip up, ever.

The snap of a twig jolted Ruby's spine straight. Okay, *that* wasn't a tiny animal. More like a large, heavy boot that had no business stalking around this lonely pocket of pasture.

Skinny tossed his head wildly and slowed his cadence. The colt's instincts were never wrong when sensing predators like bears and mountain lions, so if *he* was spooked, something was wrong.

Ruby pulled up on the reins and made soothing shushing sounds. She ran her hands over Skinny's glossy coat, debating what to do. Should she turn tail and head back? Probably an overreaction, especially since she needed to track down a herd of cattle grazing at the bottom of the trail. What would she tell the ranch's owner, Dex, if she returned to the feedlot without them? *Sorry, boss, I abandoned a hundred head of cattle because I heard a scary noise in the woods.* The thought alone stoked her pride. She wouldn't allow fear to control her—not when she'd worked for the Bureau, and not now.

Still, Skinny was having none of it. He pranced around nervously, tossing his head and pulling at his bridle like he was desperate to escape. He sensed danger lurking in those trees, and so did Ruby, judging by the icy fingers tracing a chill up her spine.

An eerie silence descended over the forest, heavy with dread. Not even an insect buzzed. It would seem every creature in the woods agreed with Skinny: something wasn't right.

Ruby peered past the thick foliage, straining against the intense afternoon sun. Suddenly, a bright white flash stabbed her eyes, blinding her.

The sun glinting off metal.

A long cylinder of metal that looked a whole lot like the muzzle of a gun.

Instinct took over. Her legs clamped hard around the saddle, and she whirled Skinny around in a tight one-eighty.

"Yah!" she cried, pressing her heels into his flanks, driving him forward. A jolt of urgency speared through her body, charging her system with adrenaline. Skinny responded instantly to her cues and the tension in her posture. He tore back down the path at a full gallop, flying around a curve...

Just as a gunshot cracked through the air.

Ruby gasped, terror flooding her body in a cold, heavy rush. She'd worked so hard to cover her tracks, to protect her true identity. The ranch's remote location seemed untraceable, its sprawling hills vast enough to shelter her from even the biggest enemy. But she'd been mistaken.

After four months of hiding, Senator Jim Walters had tracked her down.

Just like he'd hunted down her mother, an investigative reporter, for threatening to expose his secret criminal activities. A decade ago, as head of the Senate Armed Services Committee, Walters had accepted bribes by foreign entities, which he'd funneled through his "charitable" organization—The Walters Foundation—in exchange for access to government secrets. Ruby's mother, Rebecca de la Cruz, had interviewed witnesses within his organization, documenting evidence of his crimes, and was preparing to write an explosive article revealing his elicit behavior. Though Rebecca had been secretive about her work, the then-seventeen-year-old Ruby had figured out that Senator Jim Walters was the subject of her mother's investigation and that she'd begun to fear for her life.

Her mother's fears had been justified, because Walters had killed her before she could publish that article. Ruby had nearly died, too, in the fire his men had set to their home. Ruby knew Walters had ordered the hit, because he'd stood outside their house that night, his features eerily illuminated by the flames, watching. Ensuring the job was done right.

But the senator hadn't expected Rebecca's teenaged daughter to grow up and join the Bureau to gather evidence against him ten years later. Posing as an intern at his foundation, Ruby had worked her way into Walters's inner circle, witnessing enough fraudulent dealings to build a strong case against the corrupt senator. Since he'd never met her in person, he'd unabashedly bragged about his criminal exploits in front of her and his closest cronies.

Most importantly, he'd boasted about killing a meddlesome investigative journalist, Rebecca de la Cruz.

When he was charged with fraud and murder, Walters had realized, too late, that Ruby had infiltrated his foundation. Though Ruby had managed to gather some material evidence, the prosecution's case hinged on her testimony of what she'd witnessed firsthand.

Without her, the Bureau didn't have much of a case against the powerful senator, and Walters knew that.

That was why he was desperate to silence her before the trial.

Even though she was a federal agent, she and her boss had decided she would be safest under WITSEC protection. The Bureau had kept her identity hidden from the media, but Walters knew exactly who she was, and he would stop at nothing to make her meet the same end as her mother.

And with the trial only a week away, Ruby wondered if even WITSEC could guard her from the powerful senator's reach.

Case in point: the bullets flying at her right now.

Skinny raced down the narrow path glutted with rocks and roots, jostling Ruby's light frame as she clung to him tightly. Pain flared from the old burn scar on her leg, sending her crashing back through time to the flames of her burning home, her mother's screams permeating the blinding smoke. The scar covering her right calf burned like a smoldering brand, a permanent reminder of the monster who'd killed her mother.

But Ruby was no longer a frightened teen. She was a trained field agent, scrappy and tough, and the Savior was on her side. She shook off her fear before it could sink its claws into her soul and sent up a silent prayer.

Please, Lord, keep me strong so I can bring my mother justice. So I can shield others from a similar fate.

Maybe then the restless churning in her soul would find peace.

Determination steadied her racing heart and she gripped Skinny's reins so tightly her fingers ached. She drove him at a frenzied pace down the narrow, rocky trail, hooves pounding under a tangle of limbs and a cloud of dust. She prayed mindlessly and wordlessly, her brain too consumed with survival to form words. Still, her Lord understood. The woods on her left gave way to a cliff edge overlooking a wide, open prairie. Ruby glanced down the steep drop, heart hammering.

Crack. Another bullet, closer this time. Skinny let out a shrill neigh and reared up on his hind legs, pitching Ruby backward. She slid to the edge of the saddle, nearly tumbling over the side, a hundred feet of vertical drop filling her vision.

She screamed, and the horse reared up again. She clamped her body around him, holding on for dear life. Skinny was going to send her tumbling to the bottom of the valley unless she calmed him down.

But how was she supposed to do that? She was just a city girl from DC parading around as a cowgirl. She didn't know how to regain control of a hysterical horse. The ranch owner, Jude "Dex" Dexler, former rodeo champion, had taught Ruby the basics of roping and riding. For some reason, the gruff cowboy had been frustratingly protective of the only woman on his ranch and had insisted on teaching her himself.

Too bad her rodeo champion boss hadn't gotten to the chapter on controlling a bucking, thousand-pound animal. That meant she was going to have to figure this out on her own.

Her arms trembling, she wrestled against gravity, gripping the reins like a vise, and clawed her way back to the front of the saddle. Now in an upright position, she let out a shaky breath.

But if the colt tossed her back again, it could be the last time. She needed to calm him down, *now*.

"Easy, Skinny. Whoa," she whispered in his ear, her voice barely audible over the clamor of her heart. "Keep moving forward, boy." She pasted herself tight against his back, limbs shaking despite the dry, dusty heat. If they didn't keep moving forward, one of those bullets was going to hit its mark and they were going to die. But Skinny just tossed his head wildly, refusing to budge.

Despair flooded her and she threw her arms around the colt's neck, sending her desperation vibrating through the bond they shared. "Skinny, *please*."

It wasn't any of the voice commands or leg cues Dex had taught her, but somehow it pierced through the horse's panic. Skinny shot forward like a missile, jolting Ruby backward. She nearly lost her seat again, but she held fast to the reins. She tucked herself tightly against his body, clinging to him as he accelerated with an explosive power that stole her breath.

Another gunshot sailed toward them and Ruby nearly screamed with frustration. Clearly, she was dealing with a long-range assault rifle, because even with Skinny's brief delay, they'd put several hundred yards between them and the gunman. Was it possible the shooter was following them? She couldn't hear another set of hoofbeats, so he wasn't mounted. There was no sound of an engine, either, and these trails were too narrow and perilous for an ATV.

Unless there was more than one…

Maybe Walters had lined the trail with armed men? A heavy ball of dread sank into her gut. She was the Bureau's only witness, and their entire case hinged on her testimony. If she lived to tell her story, Walters would spend the rest of his life in prison. Of course he would weaponize the full force of his power to neutralize her. She was the one person in the world who could destroy him. The young, petrified teen who had watched, helpless, as his men had set the house fire that had killed her mother. The fire she'd barely escaped.

But she wasn't helpless anymore.

Her mind flew to the Winchester rifle tucked in the scabbard on her saddle. Her field agent training had assured she was a lethally accurate shot, which was why she'd avoided firing a gun since she'd arrived at the ranch. She didn't need anyone noticing how adept she was with a weapon; it would only lead to questions. But racing at this frenzied pace, firing a gun would be inaccurate at best. At worst, she'd lose her grip on Skinny and get trampled.

But accuracy wasn't needed right now; a few scattered shots might send these gunmen scampering back into the woods and buy her some time.

If she could keep her seat while she fired.

Praying wordlessly, she released the reins with one hand and reached for her rifle. It was long and awkward for someone her height, especially as she was being wildly tossed around on the saddle.

Focus, Ruby. Breathe.

She slid the weapon from its scabbard, clenching her thighs

around Skinny, hoping he wouldn't rear up on his hind legs again. If he dumped her and ran off, she'd have more to worry about than a few bruises and cracked bones. She'd be a sitting duck for a barrage of bullets.

Ruby lifted the heavy weapon with one arm, aware that aiming from this angle was a lost cause, especially with sweat stinging her eyes and the violent pounding of Skinny's hooves.

If she'd been back in DC, still working for the FBI, she would have reached for the Glock always sheathed over her hip. She recalled its perfect fit in her palm, its cool metal against her skin. She drew no enjoyment from violence, but her sidearm helped her protect others—a driving need since her mother's death.

Another shot split the air, and Ruby stopped thinking. She slid the barrel over her shoulder and shot backward, firing blind, hoping to buy time to escape.

She resheathed her weapon and pressed her face into Skinny's warm, velvety neck, moist with sweat from his frantic race down the path. She didn't know how Walters had found her, but one thing was very clear: her serene Montana refuge was no longer safe. This shower of bullets had blown her security to pieces.

God, please protect Skinny and me. Don't let me die before I've accomplished what I've set out to do.

Not before she brought down the monster who had murdered her mother and hurt so many others.

She would not allow Walters to silence her before she could deliver justice.

Dex's muscles tensed, his senses sharpening to high alert. He'd been checking the fencing around an open glen when he'd heard gunshots up on the ridge. They'd originated from a forested area edging the Oaken Trail, not far from the herd Ruby was following.

He peered through shimmering waves of heat and his eyes locked on movement on the ledge dominating the valley. A chestnut colt flew around a bend, racing down the mountain trail. The small frame of a woman clung to him, her long, midnight-black hair streaming behind her.

Ruby.

No way she'd fired those shots. He'd never seen her fire a gun, ever. Even when the other ranch hands hassled her for being squeamish and Dex offered to teach her. Dex had insisted she carry a rifle on long drives to protect the herd from bobcats and coyotes, but he'd never seen her shoot the thing once. Had she been forced to stop a predator to protect his cattle?

But a little coyote wouldn't send her fleeing at top speed like that. It was possible a hunter had wandered onto his property, but they wouldn't keep shooting if they heard a horse galloping away.

No, someone was shooting *at* her, and she was running for her life.

But who would do that? And why?

Protectiveness streaked through Dex's veins as he spun his gray quarter horse, Moody, in a hairpin turn, dug his heels into his flanks, and took off toward her like a shot across the valley.

He shouted frantic commands to Moody, his heart pumping so hard he thought it would puncture his chest. They raced across the glen in a streak of silver, hooves hammering the dry, baked earth. At this rate, they'd reach Ruby's trail in a matter of minutes. But would it be too late?

He sucked in a lungful of hot, dusty air, his throat tight. Ruby was his greenest ranch hand, small but feisty, and harder-working than any of his seasoned ranch hands. A quiet strength radiated from her; a flinty endurance that never let her admit defeat when she was learning to ride, rope and herd. Over the past four months, Dex had grown to respect her as much as any of the men working on his property, but he couldn't quell the rising protectiveness he felt toward her. He did his best to hide it—because she was proud and stubborn and likely to wrangle him to the ground if he treated her any differently than the other roughnecks he employed—but he kept an eye out for her discreetly. Only because she was new.

And for no other reason, he told himself.

The wild need to reach her clamored through him. He pressed his heels harder into Moody, pushing him to the max. Panic burned through him like a white-hot flame, knowing that, at any moment, one of those bullets could strike her. He barely repressed the illogical impulse to leap off the horse and sprint toward her, as if he could get there before his fastest mount.

Ruby was smart and brave, but she needed Dex now, and his every muscle strained to reach her.

As he drew closer, he could see her clinging desperately to Skinny, her arms and legs clamped around his back. She'd made quick progress as a rider, but she was still new. Racing at this speed, she risked sliding off and landing hard on the rocky, unforgiving path.

"Dex!" Ruby's voice carried over the narrowing space separating them, pleading, and Dex's desperation boiled over. Icy needles of fear stabbed at him, taunting him that he wouldn't get to her in time. That a bullet would blast through her and she would slip to the ground, lifeless.

"Hang on!" he yelled back, his voice rough as gravel. He would have flown to the rescue of any of his employees if they'd been in danger. But the fact that this was *Ruby* launched him into orbit.

Another *crack* exploded in the distance, flooding Dex's body with terror and rage. "Head down!" he shouted, but Ruby was already ahead of him, plastering her small frame to Skinny, ducking her head of thick, ebony hair behind the horse's broad neck.

She was less than a hundred feet away now and Dex's mind raced through possible actions. His Winchester was strapped to his back, but he couldn't risk firing with Ruby this close. He needed to put her at a safe distance before targeting the threat.

He would reach Ruby in seconds, pull her onto his horse and cover her with his own body. He slowed slightly as he approached. "Climb down," he ordered, not caring how brusque he sounded.

Apparently, Ruby didn't care either, because she raced right past, ignoring him. "Come on!" she called over her shoulder.

Dex had no choice but to follow. He whirled Moody around and thundered after her, catching up in seconds.

"I told you to dismount!" he yelled over the hammering of the horses' hooves.

"No time!" Her gaze was focused and determined. She made him think of his former teammates when he'd served as a Marine Raider—an elite special operations force. A misplaced comparison—surely this young, untrained woman had no experience with combat—but her composure under duress rivaled even the most seasoned soldiers he'd ever known.

It made him admire her even more than he already did, if that were possible.

He slowed Moody slightly, falling back so he could safely aim. He lifted his Winchester off his back and fired in the direction of the other gunshots, hoping to send the gunman into hiding. He accelerated until he caught back up to Skinny, his muscles humming with adrenaline and his nerves raw.

"Get on my horse with *me*," he shouted to Ruby over the din. He would sit her in front of him in the saddle, shielding her from behind. "One of these bullets could hit you."

"I'm aware," she responded, deadpan, and Dex couldn't decide if he wanted to scold her or gather her into his arms. Both actually. "Besides, the shooting stopped."

No guarantee that it wouldn't start back up, but she was right. The last bullet had been about a minute ago, and it had sounded farther away. They were probably out of range now.

Neither slowed their pace, though, until they reached the ranch. Dex eased Moody to a trot and ran his palm over the horse's hot, sweat-slicked hide. He leapt down and thrust the reins into the hands of a young ranch hand, Nate. "See that he gets a drink and shade. He earned it."

Dex turned to Ruby, who was dismounting Skinny. Normally, he was entertained by the sight of such a petite woman scampering down her towering mount, but he was in no mood to be charmed. He charged forward, fire rushing through his veins.

"What happened out there?" he growled, his panic morphing to anger.

She tensed, and he immediately regretted his sharp tone. He drew a deep breath and pushed a hand through his hair. "What happened, Ruby?"

Her fingers shook as she held tight to Skinny's reins. "I don't know," she murmured, her voice uneven. Now that she was out of immediate danger, her cool demeanor had cracked wide open.

Dex stepped closer and gently eased the reins from her

hand. "Tell me everything you remember," he said, less gruff this time. "From the beginning."

She looked away, her posture even more tense, and suspicion sank into his gut. She wasn't just shaken. She was cagey. Dex allowed the silence to stretch on, not pushing, but not letting her off the hook either.

"I was tracking the herd down in the prairie at the end of the Oaken Trail, when I heard movement in the trees."

"What kind of movement?"

Her hair clung in damp ringlets to her neck, perspiration pasting it to her skin. She must have been sweltering in her heavy riding clothes, exhausted and dehydrated from her heart-pumping race across the property. Still, Dex couldn't let this go. He sensed she was hiding something from him, and he wanted to make her talk before she had time to fabricate a story.

She swallowed hard, drawing Dex's gaze to the delicate shape of her neck. "I'm not sure, but it spooked me. And Skinny. When I heard the first gunshot, Skinny and I ran for our lives. And you know the rest."

She lifted her chin, daring him to press her further; which, of course, he did.

"Did you fire back?"

She hesitated, chewing on her lower lip. "I couldn't exactly hold on to Skinny and fire at the same time, so I fired backward, over my shoulder. Just to buy myself some time."

His mouth fell open and pride tugged at his heart. Even under intense fear and pressure, she'd devised a smart, unconventional solution on the fly.

"You fired your rifle backward at him? I'm impressed."

She squared her shoulders, defiant as always. "I'm not afraid of guns."

Dex's lips tipped up. "Easy, Killer. I'm saying you did good."

Her defensive mask slipped for a second and a deep well of fear shone in her eyes. She fell silent, probably unsure how to respond to praise from her relentlessly surly boss.

A pit formed in his stomach. Was he really that bad?

Yes, but he could work on his people skills later. Once Ruby was safe. "Did you get a look at the attacker?"

She tossed her hair over her shoulder. "No, I was too busy running in the other direction."

He arched a brow at her tough-guy attitude. Normally, it made him grin when she was putting one of his ill-bred employees in his place, but at the moment, he was not amused.

He tightened his grip on the reins, releasing some of his frustration on the thick leather straps. "You're acting pretty casual for someone who was almost murdered."

Those obsidian eyes of hers—the ones that could capture his fascination from across the yard—flashed with anger. "Believe me, the way I'm feeling right now is the opposite of *casual*."

Her bravado was about a quarter-inch thick and fissuring. She was scared—that much was clear—but she was also holding back something important. Dex sensed it.

"Ruby, what are you not telling me?" He practically ground the question out. It wouldn't be the first time someone with a troubled past had shown up at his far-flung ranch, looking for a new start. He didn't ask too many questions, as long as a new ranch hand worked hard and learned fast, which Ruby did. He had to admit he'd been curious about the beautiful little spitfire who'd shown up on his property with no family, no experience and only the thinnest of backstories. But he'd fallen for a beautiful city girl with secrets before and he wasn't interested in being burned again. Ruby's business was her own, and he'd resolved to stay out of it.

Until now.

She reached for the reins, but he held tight. Soft, slender fingers brushed over his and awareness shot through his haze of anger.

"Do you mind?" Her expression was tight with annoyance. "I need to take Skinny to his stall to rest."

"Nate!" he called to the ranch hand coming out of the barn. "I got another one for you."

The young man ambled over good-naturedly, asking no questions as he led Skinny away.

Ruby's jaw dropped with indignation. "He's *my* horse!"

She was right about that. Dex had found the colt months ago, lost and half starved, on the far side of the mountain. He'd named him Skinny, brought him to the ranch and nursed him back to health, but the skittish animal had refused any contact with people. So, Dex had been dumbfounded when Skinny had allowed Ruby, new at the ranch and inexperienced with riding, to fasten a saddle on him and climb up on his back. Since that day, the beautiful, damaged animal was *Ruby's* horse, no one else's. And she was his human.

"Skinny might like you the best, but he's still my horse." A low blow, reminding her that he owned everything on this ranch, but he was angry and terrified and compelled to protect this fiery, vulnerable young woman.

Against all logic.

And it was a thankless job, based on the attitude she was giving him right now. Her entire frame bristled and she glared up at him from all five feet of her. "Well, Mr. Bossman, sounds like I'm no longer needed here."

She slid her rifle from its scabbard, stepped around him, and stomped off toward the lodge. He clenched his jaw in frustration. He'd grown up on this ranch. Worked it until he'd left to serve on the Raiders, then worked it every day since his return. When his parents had retired last year and moved to Arizona, he'd taken over as owner.

He was young to run such a massive operation, but he knew what he was doing, and every single one of his big roughneck ranch hands followed his orders—except little Ruby Laurier.

And he really shouldn't adore her for it.

He opened his mouth to fire off a comeback when his eight-year-old nephew, Oliver, came tearing out of the lodge.

The little guy made a beeline for Ruby, and she set her rifle down and scooped him up in her arms.

"Ruby! Look what I made!" He waved a stick the size of his forearm, the tip honed to a sharp point. "A sword!"

Ruby grinned and hugged the little boy tight, and Dex's anger melted. Oliver's mom, Devon, had dropped him off at the ranch, begging her big brother Dex to keep an eye on him until she "figured things out"—though Devon tended to seek the answers to her problems at the bottom of a whiskey bottle.

That had been nearly six months ago, and she'd only called twice. It wasn't bills or heads of cattle or equipment costs that kept Dex up at night. It was the fear he'd have to tell that little boy that his mama wasn't coming back for him.

Dex had hired a nanny to care for the little guy while he worked; a sweet and nurturing lady in her sixties named Nancy, whom Oliver affectionately called Nanny Nan. Still, running a ranch demanded long hours, and a nanny wasn't a mother. The first couple of months his nephew was at Dexler Acres, he'd seemed adrift, emotionally unmoored by a lack of maternal love and presence.

Then Ruby had appeared like a poof of pixie dust. Much like Skinny, Oliver had immediately latched onto her, and she loved him back just as fiercely. Dex's newest ranch hand seemed to have a way with beautiful, broken things.

Maybe because she was one, too.

Ruby inspected the hand-hewn weapon in Oliver's grip. "You didn't use a knife to make that, did you?"

"Just a box cutter!" he protested, as if *that* were perfectly safe. "And Nate helped."

The young ranch hand chose that moment to reappear, only to receive Ruby's angry glare.

She was as protective as a mama bear, and Dex couldn't help but love it. Truth was, Nate loved the little guy, too. He was the oldest of several children and often took Oliver to his house to play with his younger siblings. Life could be a bit isolated for an only child at a sprawling ranch, so overnights at Nate's house were like Christmas.

Ruby rumpled Oliver's hair affectionately and set him down on his feet. "The sword looks great, Ollie Man. Just be very careful with it." She tossed Nate another lethal look. "I will talk to *you* later."

The young ranch hand lifted his hands in surrender. Seemingly satisfied, she picked up her rifle and headed for the lodge, not sparing Dex a glance. Unfortunately for her, Dex wasn't as easy to intimidate as his pubescent ranch hand. He stalked after her, eating up the space between them with his long strides. She whirled around to face him, unfazed by his simmering frustration, significant size advantage, and position as her superior.

His newest ranch hand refused to be intimidated by anyone. They had that in common.

He stepped closer, until he could see her pupils dilate in those wide, angry eyes. Close enough to notice her pulse racing at the base of her throat. He was seized by the insane impulse to fold her into his arms until her racing heart calmed. Until she felt safe.

Snap out of it. A fleeting mystery woman had deceived him before, smashing his heart to bits. He wanted none of that, ever again. He steeled himself against the rising wave of emotion that crashed into him every time Ruby was close. He would keep her safe—she was his employee on his land and therefore fell under his protection—but nothing more.

"If you're in some kind of trouble, Ruby, I need to know," he said in a low, angry rumble.

Her shoulders slumped, and just like that, the fight drained out of her. To Dex's astonishment, his words had the effect of ice water on all that fiery anger, and the expression in her bottomless dark eyes was suddenly, heartbreakingly *sad.*

"No, Dex." Her voice dropped to a whisper. "You don't want to know *this.*"

She spun away and Dex stared, slack-jawed, at her retreating back. If she had tossed him one of her saucy comebacks, he could have handled it. To be honest, he would have been reassured by a dose of Ruby's attitude.

But the despair on that pixie face *destroyed* him.

Another detail did not escape his notice: instead of heading to the bunkhouse to rack her rifle, she'd carried it with her into the lodge.

For self-defense?

Maybe his mysterious little ranch hand wasn't as squeamish about guns as she'd let on. Suspicion niggled in Dex's gut, telling him there was more to Ruby Laurier's story beneath the surface.

She was hiding a deadly secret, and it was clear she didn't want Dex's help. Unfortunately for her, he didn't plan to give her a choice. He didn't tolerate murderers lurking in his bushes. It was bad for business.

And it had nothing to do with the inconvenient ache in his heart.

TWO

Her system drenched in adrenaline, Ruby fled to her room and locked the door. Her hands shook as she fumbled for her secure phone and dialed the US Marshals Service. For the first time since she'd arrived on the ranch, she was grateful for her status as the only woman here. While the other ranch hands were piled up in the bunkhouse, Dex had provided her a private room in the lodge.

The infuriating cowboy was part bully, part protector. But for once, his insistence on her security worked in her favor.

Her witness security inspector answered on the first ring. "Greg Ward."

Her voice trembling, she identified herself according to protocol and recounted the details of her attack. Ward wasted no time with follow-up questions. Those would come later.

"I'm deploying a special operations group immediately to provide security for your transport." His tone was clipped and urgent. "They'll take you to a safe location until the trial."

That was only one week away. She needed to stay alive for a few more days then, hopefully, this nightmare would be over.

But where would they take her? Far away from this ranch she'd grown to love. Far away from Oliver. A heavy ache filled her heart. The little boy had already been abandoned by his mother. He would see Ruby's brusque, unexplained departure as yet another rejection. Emotion throbbed in the back of her throat and she wanted nothing more than to track down the little guy, pull him into her arms, and stay forever. Of course, those bullets in the woods meant that was not an option. Nor was explaining the reason she had to leave.

She would disappear, leaving Oliver wondering why she didn't care enough to stay. And Dex…her heart fluttered strangely. The handsome cowboy was gruff and overly protective, but he'd offered so much of his time teaching her about ranch life. And more than once, she'd noticed a flicker in his eyes of something *more*. Something…

But none of that mattered now. She would make a clean break, survive to testify, and return to her life in DC.

She straightened her spine and ignored the tears stinging the backs of her eyes. "When will the marshals be here?"

"ASAP, though longer than usual given your remote location. Lie low, be ready at a moment's notice and… Ruby?"

The steel in his voice made her breath hitch.

"Yes?"

"Take precautions."

She gripped her rifle in one hand, its barrel still hot from the sun. "Understood."

She ended the call and reached into the back of her closet for her go-bag containing WITSEC-issued ID cards, car keys, her Glock, and emergency cash. Her chest tightened as she looked at the clothes and personal items she was leaving behind, like a thief running off in the night. She would buy more with her emergency cash.

A nomad. No home. No roots.

She adjusted the bag's long strap snugly across her body, leaving both hands free to hold her rifle. She dragged her gaze over the bedroom she'd occupied for the last four months, a stab of longing taking her by surprise. She was a professional—a trained field agent for the FBI. She knew better than to become attached to a temporary situation. She'd spent over a year undercover with The Walters Foundation, operating under a false identity, gathering evidence against Senator Jim Walters.

She should not be feeling sentimental about a cattle ranch hideout.

Her aching heart didn't listen to her logic.

A knock on her door made her heart skip a beat. She dragged in a deep breath to normalize her voice.

"Who is it?"

"It's Oliver!"

The ache in her heart intensified to a throb. She should have told him she was busy, but she found herself opening the door.

"Hey, little man." She stepped into the hall and shut the door behind her, feeling that she was closing the door on a chapter of her life. A short chapter, but one she'd never forget.

The little boy looked up at her with his wide hazel eyes, gripping his homemade sword in his little fist. "Wanna have a sword fight?"

She sank to her knees before him, taking in his trusting, angelic features, committing them to memory. "But I don't have a sword." Her voice came out tremulous, choked with the tears she could not let fall.

"I made you one!" He bounced up and down, obviously pleased with his little surprise. "It's in the yard. Let's go get it!"

Worry leapt into her thoughts. Had he used a sharp tool to make it? Would he hurt himself playing with it?

Reality smashed into her like a wrecking ball. Soon, she would no longer be there to look out for him. He could hurt himself or feel sad or fall sick and she would never know.

A sharp ache cleaved her heart and before she could stop herself, she pulled him into her arms. It didn't take long for him to start squirming.

"Come on, Ruby! Let's go play!" He wiggled himself free of her grasp. "Why are you crying?"

Was she crying? *Stop it, Ruby.* She needed to act normal.

"Thank you, Ollie Man, for making me a sword." She wiped her eyes with the back of her hand. How was she going to explain that they couldn't play in the yard, where they were exposed and vulnerable? "You're a good kid, you know that?" She gulped in a deep breath to push down a sob. "The best."

Oliver tilted his head and stared at her. "Are you okay?"

You're scaring him, Ruby. Pull yourself together. "Yeah, I'm fine. I just..." *Can't play with you now. Or ever again.* How was she going to find the strength to reject this sweet little boy?

Sirens pealed through the air. Ruby shot to her feet, pulse pounding. The marshals couldn't already be here. It's not like they had a WITSEC office around the corner, next door to the sheriff's department.

The sheriff's department.

Dex had called the cops, and they were going to press her with questions she couldn't answer. And with the US marshals on their way, too, this was getting complicated.

Oliver was staring up at her with big, confused eyes. "Why are the police here, Ruby?"

Make that *really* complicated. How was she going to reassure Oliver when she was a knot of nerves herself?

Someone knocked at the main door to the lodge. "Ms. Laurier?" a man's voice called out. "We'd like to speak to you."

Ruby's pulse quickened and she drew a deep breath to steady her heart. *Go out there, answer their questions, and play it cool until the marshals arrive.*

She placed her hands on Oliver's shoulders. "Stay inside, okay?" She looked deeply into the little boy's eyes so he would know she was serious. "Do not come out unless Uncle Dex comes to get you." She glanced up and down the hall. "Where's Nanny Nan?"

He let out a humph. "In the playroom, picking out a book for me to read."

Perfect. He would be safe and distracted from whatever was about to happen outside. "Go see Nanny Nan, Oliver."

He stuck out his lip. "But she won't let me play with swords!"

"Wise woman, that Nancy."

She kissed the furrow in his brow and turned to leave, but his little hand wrapped around hers. "You look scared, Ruby."

Working for the Bureau, tense situations were not uncommon. She wasn't immune to fear, but she didn't let it control her. *Lord, please protect Oliver, and give me courage.*

She smiled gently. "I'm fine, Ollie Man."

She walked away, praying her little shadow wouldn't follow her. She propped her rifle against the wall just inside the doorway. Cops tended to get edgy when people greeted them with loaded rifles. Besides, she still had the Glock tucked into her go-bag.

She opened the door to find the sheriff and three deputies on the doorstep. On instinct, her eyes swept the yard and prairie beyond, scanning for threats. She doubted Walters's men would attack her with the sheriff here, but they were no doubt holed up somewhere close by, awaiting their next opportunity to strike.

"Hello, Officers," she murmured, tucking a stray curl behind her ear with shaky fingers. She didn't bother concealing the tremor in her voice. They would expect her to be shaken, and she was, so she did nothing to hide it. Dex stood behind them, tense as a bow. His gaze locked on her, concerned but also…wary. Like maybe *she* was a criminal, involved with these gunmen chasing her down. Her stomach sank. Any moment now, she would be out of his life forever and his opinion of her shouldn't matter.

Yet, for some reason, it did.

A loud gasp from behind her made her jump. She spun around to see Nancy, wide-eyed and clutching the front of her floral-printed dress.

"The police are here?" she breathed. "What's going on?"

Dex stepped forward, his posture tense. "I'll explain later, Nancy. Can you stay inside with Oliver?"

Her mouth gaping open, she nodded, stepped back and shut the door. Ruby listened as her hurried footsteps retreated.

Dex turned back to Ruby, his pale blue eyes intense, as if he could see right down into her soul. She hoped he couldn't. "I'll be right here the whole time, Ruby," he murmured, stepping beside her. "You don't need to be scared."

Of course he would act sweet and helpful *right now*, when she had to walk away forever. She drew in a fortifying breath and lifted her chin. "I'm not scared."

Humor danced in his eyes as he looked her over. "Sounds about right. But I'm still here if you need me, Killer."

She nodded stiffly, refusing to melt in the face of his gentle concern. She scanned the prairie again, her stomach twisted in knots, waiting for gunmen to materialize in the distance.

The sheriff stepped forward, flanked by his deputies. "Ms. Laurier, I'm Sheriff Liam Reyes. How are you doing?"

He looked young for a sheriff, early thirties at most, but his eyes were kind and his handsome features radiated warmth. Ruby's success as a field agent relied heavily on her ability to read people; to suss out who was lying, who was faking, and who had an agenda.

Sheriff Reyes checked out, at least at first glance. Her shoulders relaxed slightly. "I'm a bit shaken up, to be honest." No lie there.

His eyes flickered with compassion. "I imagine so." He gestured to one of his deputies, who was holding a notepad, to take notes. "Tell us what happened."

Ruby ran through her story, the same sanitized one she'd told Dex, while the sheriff's deputy wrote it all down. It was all the truth, though lacking any details that would jeopardize her true identity.

The sheriff settled a probing, though not unkind, gaze on her. "Do you know any reason why someone would target you?"

The pumping of her heart filled her ears. She needed to play the part of Ruby Laurier just a bit longer, until the extraction team got there. She could do this. "No," she said weakly, hating the lie. She was required to conceal her identity, but it didn't mean she liked the constant deception.

"So you didn't recognize the attacker?" Reyes asked.

"I never saw him. He was hidden in the woods lining the trail."

"It could have been a hunter who'd wandered onto Dex's property." Of course the sheriff would be on a first-name basis with Dex, who owned acres and acres of land in his county. "Are you certain the shots were meant for you?"

There was no denying Ruby was the target, but she was more than happy to let the sheriff believe a threat didn't exist and send him on his merry way. US marshals were due to arrive any time, and she'd rather avoid a clash with local authorities.

But Dex had witnessed the incident, and there was no way he was letting her off the hook. "The bullets were meant for her," he said firmly, holding her stare. Daring her to deny it. "The shots followed her as she ran away."

Dex stood close, his broad chest and shoulders in a protective posture. She understood that the rough-and-tumble cowboy wanted to shield her, but this bodyguard business was *not* helping.

Sheriff Reyes turned to Dex, his eyes sharp with questions. "Tell me everything you saw."

Dex described everything he'd witnessed with professional accuracy, his military background apparent in his concise details. Reyes's deputy scratched down everything in his notepad while Ruby listened, dread knotting in her stomach.

Now the cops knew this was an attempted murder and, within the hour, this place was going to be swarming with officers. They would spread out over the vast property, searching for any trace of the perpetrator. Ruby's head spun with panic. What if a news crew showed up? What if her face was flashed all over local TV screens and social media?

She scanned the long, country road leading to Dex's ranch, expecting an unmarked vehicle to appear at any moment. A WITSEC extraction team would pour out of an SUV, bundle her inside, and flee the area. What would the local police do?

What would Dex do?

She wiped her wet palms on her jeans and forced herself to think through her panic. She'd survived plenty of nerve-wracking situations while working undercover. She just needed to keep a clear head and remember her training.

While Sheriff Reyes was asking Dex follow-up questions, she discreetly slid her phone from her pocket. The other deputies probably noticed, but no one stopped her. She fired off a quick text to her witness security inspector.

Local cops are here.

No need to explain any further. Ward would notify the security team en route and coordinate with the sheriff's office to ensure a smooth extraction.

Hopefully.

Her phone instantly beeped in response.

On it. Team will be there soon.

Soon? Her body stiffened with anticipation. She'd thought it would take longer for the team to arrive, given her remote location. Everything was happening so fast, all at once. Would the sheriff and his deputies interfere with the US Marshals Service? Would Dex wrestle them down and hog-tie them? Despite herself, the thought buoyed her spirits. Her gaze traveled to her muleheaded, admittedly handsome boss, and her heart cinched.

As if he'd sensed her thoughts, he turned to her and his eyes softened. Reyes turned to her as well, his expression all business.

"Ms. Laurier, I'd like to ask you a few more—" His pocket vibrated, and he held up a finger, signaling for her to wait. He reached for his phone. "This is Reyes."

Ruby couldn't hear the person speaking on the other end, but the sheriff's eyes widened and his forehead creased with dismay. He stepped away, obviously prepared to fire off a response he didn't want anyone hearing.

Ruby had no need to eavesdrop. It was no doubt Ward, telling the county sheriff the feds were taking over this case. Reyes was facing away from her, his back stiff with anger. Clearly, the local lawman didn't appreciate the feds calling rank on him.

Dex's gaze was locked on the sheriff as well, his eyes narrowed. "Wonder what that's about," he muttered.

Ruby didn't respond, and Dex turned and studied her face…like he suspected she knew more than she was saying.

He didn't get a chance to question her because Reyes came storming back to them, shoving his phone into his pocket.

He drilled his glare into Ruby. "Where were you when the shots started?"

So, he planned to investigate the scene before federal agents arrived and booted him out. Ruby couldn't help but admire his determination. Not to mention, Reyes and his deputies leaving to investigate the crime scene served her purposes. She hardly needed an entourage of hovering protectors when the marshals showed up.

"About four miles north across this prairie, and a mile east on the Oaken Trail." She hoped he would set off in search of it right away.

The sheriff checked his sidearm, preparing to go. "You'll need to come with us and show me exactly where."

Her heart sank. She couldn't allow him to lead her away. Not when help would be there any moment.

"I'm not ready to return there. Not yet." Fear shook her words, and she didn't try to conceal it.

Reyes's eyes flashed with impatience. "I understand this is hard for you, but—"

"I'll go," Dex interjected. "I heard the first gunshot, and I know where it came from."

Of course Dex knew every square foot of his property by heart, and he could pinpoint a sound from a mile away. Ruby imagined skills like that had made him an effective Raider.

Once again, her boss was trying to protect her. Only this time, she was grateful for it. She allowed her eyes to settle on his for a moment. "Thank you."

He swallowed hard, then turned to Reyes. "You can grab an ATV parked out in the yard. I'll be right there."

The sheriff and his deputies headed toward the vehicles, but Dex hung back, trailing his gaze over her. "Ruby…" He placed his hands gently on her shoulders. "You're tense as a trigger."

The weight of his warm, callused hands felt so good, so reassuring. Still, she stepped back, out of his reach. His closeness muddled her mind and now was not the time to lose focus. Perfectly sound logic. So why did her illogical heart long to step back into his arms?

His expression fell, but he kept those keen blue eyes locked on her.

She squared her shoulders. "Anyone would be tense, given what happened."

He frowned. "Sure, but I get the feeling there's more to it."

She swallowed hard. Naturally, Dex would see past her façade. Was it his combat experience that helped him assess situations or the bond that had formed between them for the past four months? He'd spent hours with her, teaching her how to ride. He'd been surprisingly patient, considering he'd grown up riding horses, even notching three rodeo championships in bareback riding. He was naturally athletic, strong and graceful, yet he'd never made her feel self-conscious about being a beginner.

He'd never once made her feel less capable than his other hands, even if he was always protecting her behind the scenes, thinking she didn't notice.

"Dex, you are an overprotective, aggravating man." She blinked back tears welling in her eyes.

His expression softened and a grin tugged at his mouth. "Well, now that you've gotten to know me, what do you say we both go with Reyes?"

She shook her head. "I…can't right now." True statement. She tried to avoid lying, even though it was built into the framework of witness protection. And for some reason, lying to Dex felt even more miserable. She tried not to analyze the reason for that as she met his intense stare.

He dragged in a deep breath, his chest rising. "I won't leave if you don't want me to. I can tell Reyes to wait."

That wouldn't go over well with the persistent sheriff, but Dex could win a stubbornness contest against anyone, anytime. The thought would have made her grin if she wasn't so wracked with anxiety.

"No, go ahead. I'll be fine." She needed him to leave, now. So why did the thought of him walking away tear her heart to shreds?

He must have sensed her reluctance because his expression tensed with concern. He leaned forward but stopped short of touching her again. She'd backed away from him once, and Dex wasn't the type of person who needed to be told twice.

Ruby leaned toward him, too, her throat suddenly tight. Hitmen were hunting her, the local cops were pressing her for information, and a team of lethal operatives was about to usher her off to a new and terrifying unknown. Her mind was flying in a dozen different directions, but suddenly the only thing she could think of was having to walk away from Dex and Oliver.

And the thought was a hundred-pound weight on her chest.

"Dex..." Her voice was barely a whisper. "You're a good man."

The breath whooshed out of him, and he took a step closer to her. "I'll stay," he rasped, the low rumble of his voice sinking into her bones, comforting her.

She balled her fists at her sides, exasperated with herself for sending him mixed signals. She needed to convince him to leave.

"Dex, go," she said firmly.

He shook his head. "The cops can wait."

Frustration welled up inside her. "No, I need to be alone." She straightened her shoulders, steeling herself. "Stop hovering."

Hurt flashed in his eyes, and her heart cracked open. She was doing what she needed to do, but why was it so *hard*?

The vulnerability on his face shuttered over and he held up his hands. "Message received. I'll be going now."

He turned and headed over to the cops, moving with a masculine grace that made it easy to imagine him keeping his seat on a bucking bronco or driving stealthily into enemy territory.

In any case, he was walking away. Good. Now she just needed to ignore every cell in her body urging her to call him back.

She bit her lip and watched as he joined the cops at the ATVs parked across the yard. They would ride until the trail narrowed, then go the rest of the way on foot. From there, they would search the woods, looking for footprints and evidence of movement through the dense foliage.

The process would be lengthy, and by the time they returned, she would be long gone. Her mind drifted to Oliver, probably begging Nancy to play swords with him. The older woman was kind and caring but not exactly the playful type. Regret stabbed Ruby's heart as she imagined the little guy sparring alone with his little sword. Who would be his playmate once she was gone? Who would give him big hugs and muss up his hair and look out for him?

She sighed out a heavy breath and wrestled down all these emotions flying out of control. Oliver had Nate—a big brother on loan—and Dex, who watched over him and loved him like his own child. They would be fine without her.

You're doing the right thing, she told her aching heart. *This is how it needs to be.*

Movement in her periphery snagged her attention. She looked up to see a silver SUV on the horizon, headed in their direction.

WITSEC.

Her pulse pounded, and the ATV engines grumbled from across the yard. The cops were leaving, and not a moment too soon. She counted four ATVs, one for each cop as they shot across the prairie. Dex hung back, looking down at his phone. Was he dropping a pin on his GPS to send to Reyes, so the sheriff could track the location of the shooting? But wasn't he supposed to go with them?

Ruby's stomach did a flip. Her relocation team was here, and she needed to move—fast—before Dex and the cops figured out what was happening.

The cops were on the other side of the prairie by the time the SUV pulled into the drive. Without glancing back at Dex, Ruby headed toward it.

Its windows were tinted, concealing anyone inside, and Ruby slowed her step, waiting for one of the occupants to step out and identify himself.

Nothing happened.

She froze about ten feet away from the vehicle, a creeping chill winding its way up her spine. Why were the marshals not showing themselves? There was an established protocol, and they weren't following it.

Unless these weren't US marshals.

Suspicion pricked at her mind like a needle. Slowly, she walked backward and slid her hand into her pocket, where she kept her phone. Maybe she was being paranoid, but she'd earned the right. She would call Ward, confirm the location of his team—

Three men exploded out of the rear of the vehicle, spraying the yard with bullets.

Ruby dove behind a feed trough a few feet away, shots pinging off the metal. Her heart racing, she tugged her Glock out of her go-bag, slid the barrel over the top of the trough, and fired in their direction. Their barrage paused, like they'd run for cover, but one set of footsteps crunched toward her over the gravel, drawing closer.

Her pulse pounding in her ears, she gripped her weapon and readied her body to fight. She would not allow Walters to silence her, to murder his way out of the justice he deserved.

She would fight with every scrap of her strength.

Her life depended on it.

Panic and rage rushed through Dex's veins like a high-performance drug. He leaped onto an ATV and accelerated toward Ruby, his former Raider instincts kicking in even as his brain raced to catch up.

Why was an SUV full of brutes firing at Ruby?

And, apparently, she was firing back with a Glock she'd pulled out of *nowhere*.

Oh, he had a whole lot of questions for his newest ranch hand…just as soon as she was safe.

He twisted the throttle to the max, adrenaline streaking through him. Two of her attackers had scattered to find cover, one behind the open car door, another—by far the biggest dude—behind a tree, but the third crept cautiously forward, keeping his weapon trained on her hiding spot behind a trough.

Waiting for a clear killshot.

Dex reached for the rifle slung across his back and fired at the other two men, providing cover for Ruby. He wanted to aim for the guy stalking her, but she was too close to him to risk it.

Terrified he wouldn't reach her in time, Dex willed the

ATV to move faster. The gunman was only a couple feet away from her when she popped up and fired her Glock, striking his shoulder. His body whipped sideways from the force of the shot. She threw down her Glock, which must have been out of bullets, and charged him, aiming low on his body to throw off his balance.

Dex's eyes widened in disbelief. *That* was a pro move.

She tackled him down to the dusty ground, cocked her arm back and sent her fist crashing into his face. Blood gushed from his nose, which was probably broken, and she took advantage of the moment to disarm him, tucking his SIG-Sauer into the waistband of her jeans.

Dex stared at her, stunned. Impressive fighting skills from a—what had she written on her job application?—former waitress?

She'd definitely left out a few details.

But he would have time to analyze that later. He kept up his cover fire until his Winchester ran out of bullets. Approaching the scene, he didn't waste time braking. He leapt off the seat at thirty miles an hour, knowing the ATV would slow to a halt once the throttle was released, and launched himself at the largest guy.

The big goon squeezed off a couple of sloppy shots before Dex slammed into his back and gripped him in a headlock.

Dex was by no means a small man. Tall, broad-shouldered and strong from a childhood of ranch life followed by years of elite military missions. Still, when he tackled the behemoth of a man threatening Ruby, he felt like a little boy roughhousing with his daddy. The guy was a six-and-a-half-foot wall of muscle and bulk. In a contest of size and pure strength, Dex would have been trounced.

But he had an advantage: years of training that had honed him into a lethal weapon.

While the big guy clawed backward, trying to get a grip on him, Dex kept his arm locked around his beefy neck and squeezed hard. The guy resisted the pressure, flexing his thick neck muscles against Dex's grip, but Dex locked his forearm and biceps like a vise around his windpipe, cutting off his air supply. The massive beast gurgled with rage, spinning and flailing uselessly, much like a bull at a rodeo.

The former rodeo champion had an advantage there, too.

Maintaining his deadly grip, Dex's gaze bounced to Ruby. The man hiding behind the car door fired in her direction and she dropped into a roll. She popped up a few feet away from him, pulled her stolen SIG from her waistband and returned fire.

Dex's jaw was on the ground.

The man ducked back behind the car door to reload his magazine, and Ruby seized the occasion to send the heavy metal door slamming into his face, sending him reeling back.

He recovered quickly and charged, knocking both their weapons to the hard-packed ground with a dampened thud.

The fight was now hand-to-hand. Ruby ducked and dodged every blow, her movements as quick and accurate as lightning strikes. Even as Dex admired her out of the corner of his eye, his suspicion simmered. Where had she learned to fight like that? She was tiny, but fast as a feline and as skilled as any of his Raider teammates.

Her opponent lunged for her, and she dropped into a front roll, popped up beside him and sent her fist crashing into his temple.

Was it luck that she'd struck the soft spot on the side of the skull prone to concussion?

Dex doubted it.

The guy swayed on his feet, dazed, but he wouldn't give up. He lunged for her again and she hopped back, wheeled her body in a tight circle to create momentum and landed a roundhouse kick right into his ribs. He leaned forward, gasping.

Ruby was far from helpless, and yet, Dex was vibrating with the need to get to her, to fight beside her.

But this giant oaf he was battling refused to drop. Dex tightened his grip on the man's airway, choking off the thin stream of air he was still dragging in. Dex's glance shot back to Ruby, and his blood froze.

The man she was sparring with aimed a brutal kick at her knees, attempting to incapacitate her. She leapt up just in time, but he hooked her feet with his boot, sending her sprawling. She immediately rolled on her back, dodging a kick.

Dex's heart jumped into his throat. He squeezed the big guy's fleshy neck with all his strength. "Pass. Out," he growled between clenched teeth. "You big, vile—"

The goon slumped against him and slid to the ground. Dex leapt over his crumpled body and rushed to Ruby.

Her attacker loomed over her. He cocked back his foot, aiming for her head…

Dex's fury exploded. He slammed his boot into the back of the guy's knees, sending him crashing down before he even knew what hit him. He looked up in time to receive Dex's fist to his jaw, the hit so hard his head spun violently to the side. The guy struggled to his feet, his gaze glassy and unfocused, but Ruby didn't give him the chance to counter. She smashed her cowgirl boot—hard—into his knee, eliciting a roar of pain. Then she bent, plucked up his dropped weapon like a greedy little street urchin, and pistol-whipped him in the back of the skull.

Dex's jaw hung open with shock and admiration, until a flash of movement snatched his attention.

The SUV jerked forward. "Get in!" the driver screamed at his partners, who were writhing on the grass.

"Oh, no you don't," Ruby muttered, her voice vibrating with anger. She took a step toward them. To do what, Dex didn't know. Tackle them down, hog-tie them, shoot them with her newly acquired SIG? He knew his little ranch hand was feisty, but he didn't think she was reckless.

He grabbed her hand and tugged her back to him. "What are you doing?"

Her entire frame brimmed with barely restrained energy. "We can't let them get away!"

Dex's jaw dropped. "Really? Because I'd much prefer they leave."

Turns out, the driver made the choice for them. He thrust the barrel of a gun out his window and sprayed bullets in their direction.

"Take cover!" Dex pulled her behind a storage shed a few feet away and shielded her with his body.

Under the cover of the driver's gunfire, the other men hobbled back into the SUV.

"Dex, off!" Ruby mumbled, her face pressed into his cotton work shirt. "I know how to duck from bullets, geez."

His arms gentled around her, but he didn't let go. He could feel the tension in her muscles, all that fight packed into such a tiny package. Her wild mane of thick, dark hair tickled his skin, and those big, dark eyes flashed angrily at him.

"You're letting them get away!" she argued, wriggling against his grip.

So, he'd been wrong. This woman *was* reckless. "Ruby, I'm keeping you alive."

Car doors slammed, and the engine roared as the SUV accelerated out of the driveway. Dex peeked out from behind his cover to see it speed away, gravel flying from its tires.

He turned to Ruby, still crouched tensely in his arms, her expression frozen in anticipation.

Then she crumbled.

Every muscle in her body went slack and she buried her face in Dex's shoulder. The brusque one-eighty—from demanding to chase after her attackers, to *this*—was enough to make his head spin.

Dex's mind raced with questions, but for a moment, he just held her. The attack was over, and Ruby was still here, safe, with him. A wave of relief washed over him, warm and heavy and overwhelming. He tucked her snugly into his chest and let her come unraveled against him, this strong, willful person needing her one moment of weakness.

She didn't cry.

He let the moment tick by peacefully, murmuring reassuring words and smoothing her sweat-dampened hair back from her face. She didn't speak, but little by little, some of the fear drained out of those huge, dark eyes.

Dex hated to pull her back into that well of fear and tension, but he needed to know what was going on. He had to get her to talk to him.

"Ruby—"

She shook her head. "Don't."

He pressed his lips together in frustration. "I have to know what's going on."

"I already told you. You don't want to know this."

He turned her to face him. "Why?"

She pushed a heavy lock of hair out of her face and looked away. "I'm not dragging you into this."

Her answers didn't reassure him. He didn't want to believe she could be involved in something illegal. And yet…

"You've been trained to fight."

She drew a deep breath, keeping her gaze fixed far away. She didn't deny it.

That was a confirmation.

"Are you in trouble with the law?" His heart broke asking the question, but he needed to know.

She covered her face with her hands and shook her head. Was that a no or a refusal to respond?

Frustration consumed him. "Ruby." His voice was low and firm.

She looked up at him, her eyes pleading. "Dex, please. I don't want to lie to you, and I can't answer your questions."

He scanned her beautiful face smudged with dirt. A reddish-purple bruise bloomed on her right cheek, and Dex's anger boiled over. "He hit you," he rumbled.

"I hit him more." She tried to smile but winced in pain.

Dex suddenly wished he could have ten more minutes with those guys, to teach them what happens when you hit a woman. He tilted her chin up and examined the bruise. "It's swelling fast. I'll get you some ice."

She placed her hand over his wrist and electricity sizzled through him. "Will you check on Oliver?"

She locked that pleading gaze on him, and he turned to putty. He couldn't have denied her anything. "Of course," he said, his voice thick. Her hand was still on his wrist, and they were huddled so close he could see the flecks of fiery gold in her midnight eyes. "Come with me."

Her gaze wavered, and a pit of suspicion opened in his stomach. She was going to run.

Where, why, he had no idea.

She loved Oliver as fiercely as a mama bear, and even though she was reserved around his other employees, she radiated a genuine kindness that couldn't be feigned. Dex simply couldn't believe she was involved in something illegal.

Unless he just didn't *want* to believe it.

Like he hadn't *wanted* to believe his ex would lie to him and manipulate his feelings to her own benefit. She'd been a beautiful woman with secrets as well; a woman who had deceived him and ripped his heart to shreds.

He stepped back, suddenly needing space from Ruby's pretty pixie face and vulnerable eyes. "I'll go check on Oliver and bring back some ice." The gunshots had probably rattled Nancy as well, and he imagined the nanny hunkered down somewhere, awaiting an explanation.

Great.

He worked his jaw side to side, assessing Ruby. "Don't run off, okay?"

A twinkle of mischief sparkled in her eyes and, for a moment, she was that little spitfire again, rebelling against his directives. "Whatever you say, boss."

"Ruby..." His voice grumbled a warning.

She nearly grinned. Nearly. "Easy, Dex. The cops are rushing back now. They'll keep an eye on me."

He tilted his head and listened. ATV engines growled in the distance, growing closer. The cops must have heard the gunshots and turned back.

Dex shook his head, fighting back a grin. Fighting skills *and* acute situational awareness? There was definitely more to Ruby Laurier than she let him see.

And he intended to dismantle her secrets piece by piece.

THREE

"You didn't recognize any of your attackers?"

"No."

Sheriff Reyes locked his probing eyes on hers, sharp with questions. Ruby kept her posture relaxed and her expression open, skills she'd learned at the Bureau to appear calm and honest. Technically speaking, she was being honest. She didn't know who had attacked her, but she knew all too well who had sent them.

She'd already explained to Reyes that the moment he and his deputies had left, an SUV full of thugs had pulled up and attempted to kill her. She'd also informed him that she and Dex had fought them off—downplaying, of course, her fighting skills and attributing the bulk of the credit to Dex. She'd handed over the weapons she'd recovered from her attackers, but her own Glock was nowhere to be found. The thugs must have picked it up off the ground and taken it with them.

"Did you get the vehicle's plates?"

Of course she had. Like any decent field agent, she'd committed them to memory. "No."

Reyes looked disappointed but not surprised. Average victims rarely noticed helpful details.

She wasn't the average victim.

"Can you describe the assailants?"

She did, as vaguely as possible, omitting the fact that they were obviously hired muscle. Their size—especially the huge one, who was close to seven feet tall—was a dead giveaway. She wanted to lead Reyes to the conclusion that this was a random strike, maybe even a botched robbery.

As she spoke, she kept her eyes glued to the main road in the distance. When would the real US marshals be here? She'd called two hours ago. Her WITSEC placement was remote, but special operations groups were known for their lightning-fast response times.

It was the sole purpose of their existence. Getting a witness safe *as quickly as possible.*

So where *were* they?

The sheriff's eyebrows bunched together tight. "Dex said your firearms and fighting skills were impressive. Where did you learn them?"

Panic bubbled up into her throat, but she swallowed it down. "Shooting is a, uh, hobby of mine. And I've taken some self-defense classes."

Reyes glared at her. "Hmm."

Ruby's heart jackhammered, and not just because Reyes was grilling her. The marshals should have been here by now, and with every moment that ticked by, her desperation mounted. She'd called Ward, and he'd promised to get her out. The fact that Walters's men had shown up at that exact time, when she'd been expecting her extraction team, had been a coincidence.

Right?

Growing suspicion tied her gut into a double knot, but she railed against it. She didn't want to doubt Greg Ward and the US Marshals Service. Dex's ranch was remote, and it was taking them longer than usual to get here, that was all. It had to be. Because WITSEC was her one lifeline—the only defense solid enough to protect her from Walters's powerful reach.

Hopefully.

Reyes scratched his chin. "Can you think of anyone who would want to hurt you? Maybe an ex-boyfriend or someone from your past who would want revenge against you?"

She tipped her head to the side, pretending to consider that. "I haven't dated anyone in a while—" Unfortunately, that statement was all too true. "And the few relationships I've had ended on friendly terms. I moved here a few months ago, so pretty much everyone I know works here at the ranch. And we all get along fine."

Reyes sighed. "Ms. Laurier, someone tried to murder you *twice* today. You really have no idea why?" His patience was thinning, clearly. So was his faith in her story.

Ruby defended her answers, Reyes questioned her anew and they went in circles like that for over an hour. She lost track of how many times Reyes made her repeat her story—the two attacks that day as well as details of her background. She never lost her cool and stuck to her WITSEC identity, dancing around details that would compromise her cover. The sheriff asked her the same questions a dozen different ways: a strategy she knew well from working for the FBI. The mentality was, if someone was lying, they would eventually mess up.

It didn't work so well on professionals.

By the time the police cruisers pulled out of the drive that evening, every cell in her body was humming with restless frustration, and a deep pit of dread gnawed at her belly.

The US marshals weren't coming.

There was only one conclusion to draw: she'd called for help, and they'd dispatched henchmen to eliminate her.

Though her suspicion was unthinkable, she couldn't deny the reality staring her in the face: WITSEC was compromised.

And she was on her own.

She needed to get in her car and drive far away, stash the vehicle somewhere, and hole up in some dodgy hotel room until the trial. It wasn't like she could call a friend to pick her up—no one was supposed to know where she was, including her colleagues at the Bureau. Her father had passed away when she was little, and her mother had died in that fire a decade ago. She was an only child, and though she had a few distant relatives, she certainly wasn't going to endanger them by calling.

She'd never felt so alone in her life. Ruby Laurier was just a lie, a shadow, a few letters printed on fake cards. She didn't even exist.

Lord, please help me remember who I am. The child You made in Your image. Please lead me through this dark time, because I feel so, so lost.

She pulled in a deep breath and an inexplicable calm entered her body. Yes, this was hard. Her path was dark and uncertain and fraught with danger. But her Lord was with her. He would be by her side every step of the way.

She only needed to survive one more week. Then, hopefully, Walters would be taken into custody, and she could return to her life…though she didn't have much of a life to return to. Her entire existence since seventeen had been focused on justice for her mother. Once she accomplished that, what scraps of meaning and purpose remained?

But those deeper questions would have to wait. For now, she needed to flee this ranch for her own safety, as well as Dex and Oliver's.

Oliver… She hadn't seen the little guy since the police had arrived. Dex had sent Nancy home for the night. The poor nanny had been terrorized by the evening's events, despite Dex's attempts to reassure her. Dex had tucked Oliver into bed himself over an hour ago, but Ruby longed to creep inside and peek in on his angelic, sleeping face.

One last time.

A gaping hole opened in her chest, stealing her breath. She was about to walk away from that little boy, her idyllic life on the ranch and—

A tall, lean form approached in the deepening twilight.

Dex.

The dying sunset cast the farm in a deep indigo, just one shade from darkness. Gravel crunched beneath the boots of the former Marine Raider and rodeo champion, his step light and agile like a panther's.

The man knew how to handle himself; he'd proven that during the fight with Walters's men. He'd saved her life, and he deserved honesty from her. She couldn't give it to him, so she gave him the next best thing.

"I didn't thank you for earlier."

He stopped a couple feet away from her, the expression on his face unreadable in the fading light. "No, you didn't."

It wasn't a reproach; Ruby heard the humor in his voice. This man was good. Solid, strong, honest, and real. He deserved so much more than her deception. Guilt sliced through her, thinking of all the lies she'd told him. Thinking of how she was about to vanish from his ranch and his life, never having the decency to explain why.

She took a step closer, and surprise flickered in his eyes. He smelled like fresh, clean air, and warmth poured off him like a furnace. She imagined curling up into all that warmth and strength, and never leaving.

Madness.

"Dex..."

His eyes locked on hers intently, and his throat bobbed.

"You saved my life earlier."

His eyes flashed. "Happy to help. Though you were doing pretty well on your own."

He'd noticed her training, and there was no use denying it. In fact, there was no use having this conversation at all. She'd already wasted too much time dealing with the local cops, and she needed to flee before Walters's men regrouped.

And yet, she couldn't leave without talking to Dex one last time. Without saying the words clamoring to be spoken.

She settled her gaze on his, open and honest and vulnerable, and poured out the one truth she could give him.

"Thank you."

Her voice trembled as she said it, but she wasn't ashamed. For the last four months, he'd welcomed her into his home and served as her mentor and protector. A thank-you was long overdue.

"You're welcome." His voice trembled, too, though she wouldn't allow herself to consider why.

A question had been rattling around in her brain since the attack, and she couldn't walk away until she'd asked it. "Why didn't you leave on the ATVs with the cops earlier? Why did you stick around?" If he hadn't, she'd probably be dead right now.

The muscle in his jaw flickered, and his eyes burned into hers. "Because the last time you talked to me, it sounded a whole lot like goodbye."

Her heart stuttered. How could he read her so well? She was a trained field agent, experienced with undercover work. Was she really so inept at hiding her emotion?

From Dex, yes. She gritted her teeth with consternation.

He swallowed hard. "When those guys pulled up in that SUV…you were expecting them."

Her heart stopped, and her cool façade cracked wide open. She stared at him, slack-jawed. "Wh-why would you think that?" she stammered, clawing her way back to some semblance of control.

"Because you were trying to get rid of me." He took a step closer, the intensity in his eyes drilling into her. "You wouldn't come with the cops and me because you wanted to be alone. Then the SUV pulled into the drive, and you walked right toward it, as if you'd been waiting for it."

She knew her expression was broadcasting her panic, but she couldn't hide it. She didn't *want* to hide from Dex anymore.

But she couldn't very well tell him the truth, either, so she found herself staring back, speechless.

Dex pressed on. "But you wouldn't get into that car with them. They weren't who you were expecting, were they?"

The ground fell away from beneath her feet, and she was falling…

"Who *were* you expecting, Ruby?" To her surprise, he curled his palms around her upper arms gently, comforting her. "And who were the guys that showed up instead?"

She shook her head wordlessly, no longer bothering to deny his accusations. Dex was *this close* to teasing out the truth, and she needed to get out of here *now.*

His intelligent blue eyes swept over her face. "You're leaving, aren't you?"

She didn't bother lying. "I want to see Oliver one more time," she said, tears choking her words.

His jaw clenched, and he squeezed his eyes shut. "I'll walk you in."

Always the protector. But she wouldn't argue this time, since her heart was *begging* to be close to him and Oliver. Even as her logic screamed that it was time to go.

They walked in silence up the wooden steps to the lodge, then down the darkened hall to Oliver's room. Dex kept close—close enough to feel the heat that always radiated off him. Warm, solid, reliable. Ruby closed her eyes, committing him to memory.

Oliver's bedroom door was half open and she slipped inside. Her feet were silent over the hardwood floor, every breath and movement controlled. She crouched beside him and drank in his childlike features, angelic in sleep. Her heart clamored at her to throw her arms around his little body and squeeze him tight, but she wouldn't wake him. It was easier this way.

For her or for him, she wasn't sure.

For the first time since she'd vowed to God and herself that she would deliver justice for her mother, her resolve wavered. She'd spent the last decade laser-focused on one goal: put Walters behind bars for murdering her mother. So he wouldn't hurt anyone else, ever again. So no child would have to endure what she had.

Ruby believed in justice. She believed in protecting others. But her own justice was coming at a very steep cost: hurting people she'd come to care about.

She felt the weight of Dex's eyes on her from the doorway, and she sucked in a shallow, shaky breath. *Walk away, Ruby, no matter how much it hurts.*

Every moment she stayed, Oliver, Dex and everyone else on this ranch was in danger.

Guilt pressing down on her, she stood slowly and dragged herself to the door. Dex stood just inches away from her, tension vibrating between them. In the darkness, his eyes were twin pools of navy blue, deep and sober.

"You don't need to leave," he told her.

His low voice rumbled through her like a warm, comforting wave. She closed her eyes, fighting the temptation to lean into his solid presence. "Yes, I do."

He frowned. "What kind of trouble are you in?"

The suspicion on his face shattered her. He probably thought she was involved in something illegal. Why else would a carful of thugs show up to kill her?

"Whatever you're thinking, it's wrong." She was saying too much. She needed to extract herself from this tangle of emotion before she compromised everyone's safety. "Thank you for…" *Welcoming me into your home. Teaching me everything I needed to know about ranching. Trying to protect me.* "…For everything."

She turned on her heel to head out before she could say something she would regret. She touched the go-bag still strapped across her middle, ensuring she had her fake ID cards and enough cash to last until the trial.

Emptiness opened inside her like a yawning vacuum.

She strode toward the front door, aware of Dex's quiet footsteps behind her. For a man his size, he was light on his feet, even in boots. He walked like a feline stalking its prey: controlled, graceful, brimming with tightly coiled power. And even though she hadn't admitted it, the way he'd leapt off that moving ATV and grasped her attacker in a choke hold was one of the most impressive things she'd ever seen. And she'd seen a lot.

She stepped onto the porch, warning herself not to look back, but her heart disobeyed. Slowly, she turned until she was face to face with Dex. His tall, muscular frame filled the doorway, the rugged planes of his face sharp with tension. He curled his fingers over the top of the doorframe, as if to keep them from reaching out to her.

"I'm here if you need me." His voice came out rough as gravel.

So, he wasn't going to try to stop her from leaving. To her surprise, disappointment rattled her resolve. She hadn't been hoping her overly protective, intrusive boss would stand in her way, had she?

Against all logic, this sudden respect for her space and independence made her long to stay.

Stop being ridiculous. You wanted him to back off, so he did. Now get in your car and leave already.

She hoped he couldn't see her unshed tears in the gloomy glow of dusk. She squeezed her eyes shut, trying to contain them. "Goodbye, Dex."

His chest rose sharply, and he cleared his throat. "Goodbye, Ruby."

She couldn't stare any longer into that ruggedly handsome face marked with hurt and concern. She spun away and walked down the steps, her legs like lead.

You're doing the right thing. You're keeping everyone safe. If you stay, you'll only bring them more trouble.

The sage little voice in her mind played nonstop on a loop as she walked to her car, boots crunching over the gravel drive. The heaviness in her chest made it hard to breathe, and warring emotions tugged at her mind. Why was she acting so sentimental? She'd trained for these situations. She'd infiltrated The Walters Foundation for over a year, meeting people, earning their trust, walking away. Why was it different this time?

Her gaze snagged on the indigo outline of the mountains in the distance, the tall grasses of the prairie swaying in the cool evening breeze. She thought of Oliver tucked in tight and warm in his little bed.

Of the good and caring man still standing in the doorway, watching her leave.

In her heart, she knew what made this time different. It was in her heart and all around her.

This place had become her home.

Swallowing down the heavy knot in her throat, she pulled her keys from her purse. *Get in the car, Ruby. Drive away.*

Her spirit heavy with regret, she climbed into the car and shut the door. It was a battle of wills to not look out the driver's-side window—a battle she lost. Dex still stood in the same place, frozen like a tall, handsome statue. This was his silent protest. His statement that he would be right here, waiting, if she changed her mind.

Despite herself, her heart fluttered with a spark of hope. Maybe, after the trial, if everything worked out, she could come back…

Ridiculous. How would that conversation go? *Hi, Dex and Oliver, I'm back. Oh, and by the way, I've been lying to you for the past four months. I put you in danger to keep myself safe. So, you cool with me moving back in?*

Ruby shuddered to even contemplate that. No, it was best she moved on. For everyone involved.

Before she could turn away, Dex's eyes locked on hers. From this distance, in the murky light, she couldn't see them as much as feel them. He raised his hand in farewell, but her hands were shaking too much to return the gesture. Her trembling fingers fumbled to insert the key into the ignition. Finally, it slid in and she twisted it with a flick of her wrist.

Nothing happened.

The car was silent, except for a soft click activating some mechanism under the hood. Ruby's field agent brain raced so fast, the next second ticked by in slow motion. She gripped the door handle with one hand. Shoved the door open with the other.

Then she dove.

Cool, night air rushed over her skin as she launched herself out of the vehicle just as the engine exploded in a deafening blast. She was blinded by white-hot flames lighting up the night like the noon sun, the searing heat burning through her clothes, singeing her hair and skin. The rock-hard ground rushed up to meet her as she curled into a tight ball, rolling several feet away.

Excruciating pain shot up her left ankle—she must have twisted it as she'd leapt out—and the ribs on her left side screamed in agony. The side of her body that had absorbed the fall felt cracked into pieces, but adrenaline prevented her from dwelling on it. She needed to put more distance between herself and the raging flames.

She pushed herself up on her elbows and crab-walked farther from the scalding heat pouring off her car. Even from a few feet away, the intensity of the blaze seared her skin. Her old burn scar—from the fire that had killed her mother—flared with pain, like a brand on her skin. On her soul. She shook her arms and legs, trying to release the fiery heat trapped inside her clothing.

Thick plumes of smoke choked the air around her, filling her lungs with burning, toxic ash. She was instantly seized by violent coughs, and her eyes stung and watered. She jerked her arm up to cover her face, and knives of pain stabbed her shoulder. She must have hurt that, too, when she'd landed.

Father, I can't breathe. I can't...

Memories of that deadly fire, ten years ago, slammed into her. Her mother screaming, trapped behind a collapsed section of the ceiling. Ruby trying to reach her. The blinding agony of flames licking her calf, melting her skin, leaving a scar that would never stop burning. Firefighters in masks reaching for her, pulling her out.

Sorry we couldn't get to your mom in time. So sorry...

The old grief resurfaced, new and raw again, dragging her down and drowning her. Crazed with panic, she scrambled backward, desperate to escape the unbearable heat and smothering smoke.

Over the roar of the fire and the noise in her mind, she processed footsteps pounding toward her.

Dex.

Relief washed over her in an overwhelming rush. Tears slid down her scorched cheeks, and sobs choked her.

Do not lose it in front of him, Ruby. Act strong—

His arms wrapped around her, and she was instantly lifted into the air, tucked into his chest as he carried her away from the blinding, burning heat. She squeezed her eyes shut against the dizzying pain on the left side of her body, but the brilliance of the flames shone through her closed eyelids.

You're not back in that fire again, she told herself, her logic battling the raw emotion of her memories. *You're okay. You're okay. You're—*

"You're okay, Ruby." Dex tucked his face against her cheek so she could hear him. "I've got you."

The iron clamp around her lungs loosened ever so slightly. She opened her mouth to respond, but hacking coughs choked her. She struggled to draw a breath between spasms, her head swimming from lack of oxygen.

"Try to calm your body." Dex's tone was comforting but firm. Ruby imagined him in active combat situations, staying calm and focused to accomplish a mission.

And she was suddenly, desperately, grateful he was there with her.

And grateful for her own training, which slid into place as the mindless panic drained away. She concentrated on slowing her pulse and relaxing each muscle group, one at a time.

She pulled in tiny sips of air between each violent cough, just enough to keep her head clear, even though her body demanded more.

"That's it, Ruby." Dex rubbed circles over her back, his hands firm but gentle. "Coughing is good. It's clearing your lungs. Just take the breaths you can."

By the time they'd reached the porch, the coughs were coming less frequently, and she drank deeper from the cool, clean air. Dex set her on a wooden deck chair and kneeled in front of her.

Ruby watched, astonished, as he swept a panicked look over her, searching for injuries. He'd seemed so calm and controlled a moment ago, swiftly removing her from danger, then calmly coaching her to regain her breaths. But now, he was running a wild gaze over her like she might shatter into pieces. She supposed the reaction harkened back to his training as well: act first, freak out later. It was a mantra she'd lived by in the Bureau, too.

"I'm…" Her voice snagged on a cough. "Okay."

His chest caved, like he was relieved to hear her voice, but also unconvinced. "Are you hurt?"

Adrenaline was fading from her system and mind-numbing pain rushed in to take its place. "My left side," she said between her teeth, "where I landed."

Dex ran gentle fingers over her shoulder and down her side, making her wince. "Your shoulder is probably just bruised, but your lower left ribs feel swollen." His gaze traveled down her hip and leg. "Is it all right if I check this, too?"

She nodded stiffly, pain stealing her breath.

He gingerly palpated her hip and leg. "Hurt?"

She shook her head. "I wrenched my ankle jumping out of the car though."

Dex frowned. "It's going to swell up, too, so it's better to take your boot off now."

"O-kay," she huffed, her body throbbing so fiercely it was hard to put words together.

Slowly, he eased the boot off her foot. She grimaced as the stiff leather pressed into the painful joint, sucking in a gasp of agony.

"Sorry." The low timbre of Dex's voice was lethal. It was clear in his tense posture and vibrating energy that he wanted to get his hands on whoever had done this to her. But he was prioritizing her care right now, and she could have wept with appreciation.

When was the last time someone had taken care of her?

Her mother. Ten years ago.

Had it really been a decade since someone had cared about her? That must be why she was dissolving into a weeping mess, because Dex was showing her some kindness. Shame swept through her, making her skin flush. She was being weak; instead of distancing herself from the people she cared about, she was putting them in danger by staying. By needing them.

But how was she supposed to leave now, with no car? Limp away on her sprained ankle?

She let her face fall into her hands, despair sweeping over her. How was she going to survive until her trial? How was she going to remove herself, Dex, and Oliver from Walters's grasp?

"Ruby..." Dex's low voice rumbled gently over her. He took both her hands in his and brushed his thumbs across her knuckles. "Ruby, it's going to be okay."

Hot, salty tears spilled down her cheeks. She should have let go of Dex's hands and covered her face, but honestly, his touch warmed the chill spreading through her.

"I'm so sorry," she choked out.

The breath whooshed from him. "Sorry? Ruby, no. None of this is your fault—"

"It is." Her voice steadied, and the words came out stronger. "I've put you and Oliver in danger by being here."

His expression tensed. "If you would just tell me—"

"Dex." She dragged in a rattly breath. Her voice was scratchy and raw, but she needed to get these words out. She needed him to understand her boundaries. "It's safer if you don't know."

His entire body was so tense with frustration, he looked ready to explode. Ruby closed her eyes and let her head drop into her hands again. She was so weary. Weary from running. Weary from looking over her shoulder every moment. Weary from arguing about this with Dex. The weight of all her secrets was crushing her.

Still, coming clean with Dex was not an option. She'd heard stories of witnesses blowing their covers, and it did not end well—for them or the people they'd burdened with their secrets. She was tempted to contact her boss at the Bureau, but if the US Marshals Service was compromised, the FBI could be, too. As unfathomable as that scenario seemed, instinct told her to fly under the radar until she'd fled her compromised hideout. Maybe then she would reach out in a way that felt safe.

For now, her only choice was to run from the ranch and Dex and everything she held dear. It ripped her heart in two, but it was the right thing to do.

But where would she go? How would she get there without a car? There was no way Dex would drop her off at a bus station and drive off.

That's it! An idea flashed through her mind, lighting a way forward.

The plan might work, if she could just figure out a way to slip between Dex's fingers…though she had a feeling he wouldn't make it easy.

"Tell me who keeps hurting you," Dex demanded, his patience about as thick as a toothpick. In his defense, it was the fifth time he'd asked. And that didn't count all the times the first responders had asked her, too.

He'd of course called 9-1-1. Firefighters had arrived to extinguish the car fire, paramedics had checked Ruby's injuries, and cops had investigated the scene and asked questions. Unfortunately, they hadn't uncovered anything more than what Dex had already surmised: someone had planted an improvised explosive device under the hood of Ruby's car, detonated by the starter. No one knew who or why, or how they'd placed the bomb without anyone noticing. Ruby hadn't driven the vehicle in days—she lived on the ranch and only left once or twice a week for church and to buy provisions in town. The bomb could have been there for days.

Long story short, they had more questions than answers, and Ruby wasn't cooperating.

Surprise, surprise.

Ruby shook her head, wincing from the movement. "I've already told you I can't."

"Ruby, you're in trouble." He'd settled her into a recliner in the living room, where she insisted on keeping her rifle propped up beside her. Dex hated that his presence alone wasn't enough to make her feel safe, but danger electrified the air around them. It was in the curls of smoke wafting past the windows, the trembling of her fingers, the tension in Dex's muscles. Someone wanted to kill her, and she was too proud—or too afraid—to let him help.

Not to mention, helping her was putting them all at risk…

including his young nephew he'd promised to protect. He wanted Oliver as far away from danger as possible, but a pull on his heart demanded that he protect Ruby, too. His soul was flooded with an inexplicable need to look out for her; an instinct so strong he knew it exceeded his own will. The Lord was urging him to keep Ruby close; a command that his own heart was all too happy to obey.

He looked her over now, protectiveness streaking through his veins. She had ice packs on her head, her shoulder, her ribs and her ankle. Her entire left side was bruised and tender, though paramedics had determined that she hadn't broken any bones. Dex looked her over, his chest tight. "Ruby, you've got a concussion, banged-up ribs, a sprained ankle, and I'm running out of ice packs."

She cracked open an eyelid and glared at him through the glassy slit. "Thanks for the evaluation. Why would I need a doctor when I've got you?"

A growl escaped his throat. "You know more about these attacks than you're saying. Why won't you talk to the cops?" He swallowed hard. "Why won't you talk to *me*?"

Probably because she was scared out of her mind and unable to trust anyone right now. The thought made Dex ball his fists at his sides. She could trust *him*. He could keep her safe. But how could he convince her of that?

She closed her eyes, obviously exhausted and hurting. "I'm perfectly fine."

"You're perfectly stubborn."

"Thanks for noticing."

Dex was normally a cool-headed guy, but Ruby Laurier had a talent for whipping him into a froth.

Because you care about her. Because your emotions are all tangled up in this feisty, spirited woman who would do anything to hide how vulnerable she is.

Like she could sense his turmoil, she opened her eyes. "You're sweet to worry about me."

Sweet? That was a compliment he'd never received before, from her or anyone else. He was a surly grouch with the habit of giving orders. Of course, for her, his insides were soft teddy-bear stuffing, but he'd hidden that well.

Hadn't he?

The softness in her eyes suggested she might be on to him, which made his spine stiffen. If she had any idea what a pushover he was for her, he was *toast.*

"You take good care of me, Dex," she whispered.

"You don't make it easy, Killer." His voice came out thick with emotion, which annoyed him.

"Never said I did." She grinned, lowered her feet to the floor and slowly stood. "Now, if you'll excuse me, I need eight hours in a bed."

Dex agreed, but he didn't trust her to stay put for eight hours. Beneath her bravado, she was tense with fear. He'd caught her looking out the window every minute, scanning the roads and the yard. She knew her attackers were still on the hunt, and she wasn't about to drift off to sleep any time soon. She was going to make a run for it, and Dex planned to do everything short of hog-tying her to prevent it. Not that hog-tying wasn't tempting, but he couldn't force Ruby to stay. She was an adult with her own free will, and if she wanted to do something foolish like run off on her own, he couldn't stop her.

Didn't mean he wouldn't try though.

"I'll put some fresh ice in those packs for you." He plucked the abandoned compresses from the recliner and headed for the kitchen.

"Thank you." Ruby picked up her gun and slowly headed

down the hall to her room, too proud to limp, but Dex didn't miss the lines of strain on her face.

This woman was more muleheaded than he was, and that was saying something. It exasperated him beyond words and made his heart ache all at once. Because this brave, willful young woman shouldn't have to be this strong just to survive.

Dex found himself dreaming about being her hero, and he needed to crush the rising fantasy before it swayed his logic. He'd sworn off mysterious women who kept secrets from him. He'd played that game before and gotten burned. So the fact that he felt irresistibly drawn to Ruby frustrated him.

He would bring her the darn ice packs—and some extra painkillers, he thought as he plucked the bottle from the kitchen ledge—and try his reasonable best to keep her out of trouble. Nothing else. No feelings involved.

The door to her room was half open, but he knocked anyway. She came to the doorway, gun in her hand and a contrite look on her face, and took the ice packs from him. "You're too nice to me."

"Yes, I am."

She chuckled, and the sound was so sweet, Dex wished he heard it more often. "Those painkillers kicking in yet?"

"I think so." She yawned into her fist and offered him a sleepy grin.

Since her hands were full with ice and guns, he walked into her room and placed the bottle of pain meds on her nightstand. "You're gonna need more at some point in the night."

Her expression softened, and he cleared his throat, ignoring the warm feeling fluttering through him. He gestured toward the rifle. "You going to sleep with that thing?"

Her grin dissipated. "I'm going to keep it close."

He pursed his lips. "I'll keep close, too. I won't let anything happen to you."

Her eyes widened, and her cheeks colored. Clearly, she wasn't used to people looking out for her. Or maybe she wasn't used to him being nice. He winced. He really did need to soften his hard edges.

Silence hung in the air and he clenched his jaw against all the words threatening to spill out of his mouth. "Well, good night." He strode out the door, but not before he caught a spark of sadness in her eyes.

"Good night, Dex." She shut the door.

Yeah, she was definitely going to run.

But not if he could help it.

He returned to the living room, gripped the recliner by the arms and dragged it noisily into the hallway between Ruby's and Oliver's rooms.

Her door flew back open, and she appeared in the doorway, muscles tense. "What are you doing?"

Didn't think I'd be keeping vigil outside your bedroom, did you, sweetheart? "I said I would keep close. To you and Oliver." His pistol was holstered over his hip, loaded and ready. He wouldn't be getting any sleep tonight, but that didn't worry him. Sometimes Raider missions had demanded that he go nights on end with minimal sleep. It wasn't much fun, but he'd learned to compartmentalize the fatigue and still perform.

He'd also asked Reyes to send deputies to check on the ranch overnight, and the sheriff had promised to make hourly passes. Hopefully, the presence of police cruisers would deter any more attacks.

And if it didn't, Dex would be ready to defend Oliver, Ruby, and his property.

Ruby watched from her doorway, stiff as a board, as he settled into his chair. Uncertainty flickered in her huge, dark eyes, and Dex's suspicions were confirmed. *It's going to be a bit harder to slip out of here, unnoticed, with me posted outside your door, won't it?*

Her glance flicked to Oliver's room and she let out a shaky breath. "I'm glad you're sticking close."

Dex's pulse accelerated. She was glad he was sticking close to *Oliver*, not her, but his heart interpreted it the way it wanted. "I'm here if you need me, Ruby." He let his gaze sink into her wide, onyx eyes. "Right here."

Her lips parted and for a moment they stared at each other in silence. "I know," she finally said. Her obstinate expression fell, and for a moment she looked so vulnerable and so *afraid*, his heart broke. "Thank you."

He was seized with a wild impulse to gather her into his arms, thread his fingers through her silky, dark curls, and tell her everything was going to be all right.

Bad idea.

Dex needed to protect her, but he also needed to protect his heart *from* her. She was going to walk away from him—if not tonight, then soon—and he intended to keep his heart in one piece. And that meant keeping his distance from this magnetic force pulling him toward her.

He didn't need to battle the impulse for long. With one long, last look, Ruby closed her door, shutting him out. Dex stared at the closed door for a moment, pulling himself together. *You are* not *falling for your troubled employee.* He repeated it in his head until he'd nearly convinced himself. Oliver stirred and mumbled something in his sleep, and Dex's chest tightened. Danger pressed in from all sides, relentless and threatening. These two people he cared about were surrounded by his walls, tucked snugly in their beds, but Dex held no delusions about their safety. Even with Reyes's deputies patrolling and Dex standing guard, the threat was out there. Lurking.

Lord, please watch over Oliver and Ruby. Keep me strong and alert so I can protect them.

Because whoever was after Ruby was no doubt nearby, awaiting their next opportunity to strike.

FOUR

Ruby had been lying stiff as a board in her bed for the past hour and a half, ears peeled for the slightest sound or movement. The meds she'd swallowed had dulled some of her pain, but her entire left side still throbbed. The ice in her packs had warmed a while ago, but she didn't want to limp back to the kitchen for more. If Dex had fallen asleep—which she desperately hoped—she didn't intend to wake him.

The lodge was silent, save for the cicadas buzzing outside her window. She'd left it open, and not for the cool night breeze. She planned to slip out the window once Dex fell asleep, and she couldn't risk waking him by sliding it open.

Trouble was, she couldn't tell if the vigilant former Raider had dozed off or not. Except for the occasional creak from his recliner, he didn't make a sound. Ruby would not have put it past him to stay awake all night, babysitting her.

Her simmering frustration was accompanied by a swell of gratitude. Dex was doing everything in his power to look out for her. He just couldn't get it through his thick skull that she was protecting him and Oliver by leaving.

She hoped he was asleep, because she couldn't wait any longer to carry out her plan. Walters's hitmen could make a move at any moment, and she would be a coiled ball of dread until she was a hundred miles from here.

Ruby pushed herself up from the bed and pain seared through her left side. She ignored it and crept to the window, her twisted ankle protesting. She'd placed her go-bag near the ledge, along with the keys to Dex's truck, which she'd lifted from the hook earlier. Guilt weighed heavily on her at the thought of taking his truck, but she wasn't *stealing* it. Once she got to the bus station fifteen miles away, she would text him the location where it was parked.

Swallowing past the knot in her throat, she slung her bag over her good shoulder and grabbed her rifle. She grasped the keys between her fingers so they wouldn't jangle and eased her body out the window, babying her left side as much as possible. It was only a two-foot drop to the grass below, and she didn't make a sound.

Her feet were silent over the hard-packed dirt as she carefully limped to Dex's old manual transmission pickup truck parked in the gravel drive. Knives of pain stabbed at her ankle, reminding her to purchase an ankle brace at the earliest opportunity. She opened the driver's-side door, deposited her gun and bag on the front passenger seat, and slid the gearshift into Neutral. Now for the really painful part. She went around to the back of the truck, gritted her teeth and pushed. Her entire left side felt like it was ripping apart at the seams, her tender shoulder joint and ribs screaming in pain. Still, she pushed with all the strength in her small frame.

Once these painkillers wore off, she was going to regret this.

But she had no choice. Slowly, Dex's truck crawled forward and gained momentum. She jogged back up to the front and turned the steering wheel slightly, correcting its path down the driveway. Soon, she reached the road. Ruby turned the steering wheel sharply and pushed some more, her body protesting, until she was about fifty yards down the road. Then she hopped into the driver's seat.

Now for the really scary part. There was no way to silently start the truck, and if Dex heard the engine roll over, he'd chase after her in one of his other vehicles. And she didn't even want to imagine how furious he would be. She just had to hope that she was far enough away that he either wouldn't hear it or would think it was just another car on the road.

Ruby steeled her nerves and pushed down the clutch with her injured left foot, wincing against the pain. She twisted the key in the ignition and terrifying images of her car's explosion leapt into her head, paralyzing her. She hadn't stopped to think that Walters might have rigged Dex's truck, too…

But the engine purred to life, normal as a Wednesday.

Releasing a tremulous breath, she threw the truck into Drive and hit the gas. Her head pounded, and her left shoulder and ribs felt like she'd injured them all over again, but she breathed through the fiery pain until it settled. She would be sore for a while, but she would survive. She always did.

The bus station was only twenty minutes away, but it was the middle of the night, and she would need to wait until the first bus left in the morning. She had no idea where it was headed, but she did know one thing: she would be on it.

She drove down the ink-black highway, the truck's headlights her only light out here in the country. A blanket of clouds concealed the moon and stars, creating near-total darkness, and Ruby felt like she was barreling toward an abyss. She wondered whether Walters's men were still lurking around Dex's property or if they'd seen her slip away. She prayed they would leave Dex, Oliver, and everyone else at the ranch in peace now. She checked her rearview mirror every five seconds, expecting to see headlights pursuing her in the distance.

There was nothing but pitch-black night surrounding her. Like she was the only living being for miles.

And she felt so alone.

Father, I know You're here with me, she prayed, *even when I can't see You.*

Her faith fortified her, scattering her fear like shadows under a beam of light.

There was a twenty-four-hour gas station and convenience store ahead, and Ruby knew they had a rack of prepaid phones for sale. She would need to ditch her current phone, in case it was being tracked, and use burner phones instead. She slowed Dex's truck as she approached the gas station, noting there were no other customers at this time of night. The lights were on inside the convenience store, and a woman stood behind the counter, looking bored. Ruby glanced at the illuminated time on the dash: 1:42 a.m.

Ruby drove past, did a U-turn and circled back. She pulled into a spot on the side and put Dex's truck into Park.

Her heart raced, and she considered abandoning her idea completely. What if one of Walters's men had followed her, planning to attack her once she stepped out of the truck? She checked her windows and mirrors for the hundredth time and decided to risk it. She needed multiple burner phones for internet access and in case of emergencies. She glanced at the rifle propped against the passenger seat, wishing she still had the Glock she could conceal inside her bag.

She was going to have to walk in that store unarmed and pray for the best.

Snatching her bag off the seat, Ruby gingerly slid out, clenching her jaw against the pain. Her pulse thundered past her ears as she stepped into the store, trying not to limp, because that was a detail people remembered.

She blinked against the glare of the artificial lights and

glanced at the clerk behind the counter. The woman gave her a polite smile and Ruby nodded, her muscles tight. She located the rack of prepaid phones and grabbed two, wanting to take more but not wanting to draw attention. She would buy two more at the next opportunity. She made a quick tour around the store, selecting a few provisions: some bottled water, a few protein bars, and some cold-brew coffee. She looked longingly at the hot, freshly brewed coffee at the self-serve station, but she had no time for the luxury. The bottled stuff would provide quick and simple caffeine to keep her alert. She grabbed three bottles of it and headed to the counter with her loot.

The clerk reached for her barcode scanner gun. “Stocking up for a long night on the road?”

Ruby tensed. The woman was probably just making small talk, but Ruby wanted to keep all contact with strangers to a minimum. If Walters or his men came by asking about her, she wanted to be as unmemorable as possible.

She kept her eyes down and her voice low. “Yeah.”

The woman took the hint and stopped making pleasantries. She finished scanning the items and placed them in a bag.

Ruby looked at the price displayed digitally on the register and paid with cash. She barely took the time to accept her change before she headed for the door, forcing a natural gait even though every step was agony.

She hobbled back to the truck, keeping her eyes peeled to the shadows. An SUV rushed by on the highway, and she nearly leapt out of her skin. Was it Walters? Had he hunted her down?

But the SUV kept going. Ruby practically dove back into Dex’s pickup and jammed her thumb down on the lock button. Breathless with fear and pain, she tossed her bag of supplies on the seat next to her and fired up the truck. Once she was back on the highway, a mile down the road, her breaths calmed.

You're okay, Ruby. You're going to make it.

The bus station was only a couple of miles ahead, but she wouldn't risk parking there all night. That was too long to linger anyplace, especially since Walters would be expecting her to flee, and the bus station was an obvious start.

The station came into sight, its parking lot dark and empty. Ruby scanned the surrounding area. A county road off to the right melted into the distance, lined with woods.

Perfect.

She turned onto the deserted road and drove until she found a gravel pull-off. She steered the truck around a curve that led to a small picnic area and parked behind a cluster of trees. No one would be able to spot her from the road, and there was nothing behind her but woods and a stream. Ruby imagined a happy, outdoorsy family picnicking there, calm, contented and together, and her heart ached. Would she ever have that sense of safety?

Would she ever know what it was like to have a family?

Growing up, it had been just her and her mother, Rebecca. Her father had died suddenly of a congenital heart condition when Ruby was little, and she hardly remembered him. After her mother's death, she'd stayed with a distant relative for a few months until she'd turned eighteen and graduated high school, but she'd never been close to any of her parents' relatives. They lived far away and had their own busy lives. Ruby used to visit on holidays, but she hadn't even done that for the past three years.

Maybe, if she survived this nightmare, she would start over. She would return to the church she'd attended before she'd gone undercover. She would join groups and make an effort to connect with others. She'd always wanted to have people in her life she loved and trusted, but her single-minded need for justice clashed with the demands of a close relationship. Working undercover was hardly conducive to dating, since she couldn't tell anyone who she really was. Life in WITSEC posed the same problem: any relationship she might have developed would be based on a lie. Besides, she was so focused on her job, she lacked the bandwidth for a romantic attachment. Once Walters was behind bars, where he couldn't hurt anyone else, maybe…

She would think about all that later.

Ruby pulled out one of her prepaid phones and checked the bus schedule. The first route leaving town was at 6:00 a.m., headed for Casper, Wyoming.

Casper it is.

She would park Dex's truck at the station and text him its location right before she boarded the bus. Once she was in Casper, she would buy a ticket for another place. Didn't matter where, as long as it was far from here, where Walters couldn't track her. She consulted the time again. Almost 2:00 a.m. Nothing left to do now but wait.

Sitting in tense silence, Ruby trained her eyes on the shadows. Time ticked by slowly, like mud drying in the sun, every minute an agony without the slightest distraction. At one point, almost an hour passed in an instant, and she realized she'd nodded off. Panicking, she reached for a bottle of cold brew and chugged half the contents. The pain in her shoulder and ribs ignited at the sudden movement, but she held back a gasp and swallowed the caffeine. The oblivion of sleep would have offered a reprieve from this constant, burning pain, but she couldn't afford that luxury right now. Maybe once she arrived in Casper, she'd take some of the pain meds she'd tossed in her go-bag and doze on the next bus ride. She was bone-weary and running on fumes, but until she was far from the ranch, she needed to stay alert.

After what felt like an eternity, dark purple, like a bruise, smeared the inky-black sky. A faint glow grew from the east, and Ruby checked the time on her phone: 5:32 a.m. Time to go.

Starting the engine, she threw the gearshift into Drive, her shoulder protesting, and pulled back out onto the road. She arrived at the station a few minutes later and parked. Her field agent brain cataloged the four other cars in the lot along with their license plates. Unfortunately, she would need to leave the rifle in the truck. It belonged to Dex, and it was too big to conceal, anyway, but the idea of walking out into the open, unarmed, made her heart pound like a drum.

She stuffed her plastic grocery bag of provisions into her go-bag, dropped the keys in the cupholder, and locked the door. She wouldn't message Dex right away. She couldn't risk him showing up here, demanding answers.

She stepped inside the station, processing every detail of her surroundings, from the woman behind the counter, to the other travelers waiting in vinyl seats, to the emergency exit in the back of the building.

Purchasing her ticket with cash from her bag, she glanced at the time. Five fifty. The bus was scheduled to leave in ten minutes, and the first passengers were already queued up outside to board. Time to send a text to Dex, then drop her phone into a garbage bin.

She headed for the ladies' room, pushed open the door and locked herself inside. There was one stall, a sink, a mirror, and an exterior door at the rear. The space had seen better days, but she wasn't there for the décor. She just needed a quiet spot—alone—to send Dex this final message. Her hands were slick with sweat, her fingers fumbling as she struggled to type.

I borrowed your truck to drive to the bus station. The keys are locked inside. I'm sorry.

Her fingers paused over the screen. Dex deserved so much more than this hasty, inadequate message. He'd done so much for her; more than she'd deserved. Her mind raced with all the words she couldn't say, until she blew out a breath and gave up.

Thank you, she added, and tossed the phone into the garbage.

The phone sank beneath a pile of damp paper towels, and Ruby's heart ached so fiercely she thought it would burst. She felt she'd just tossed Dex himself into the trash—and Oliver, too—like temporary things she'd used up and discarded. How had her life come to this? A bus station bathroom, the only people she'd cared for in years thrown away and forgotten?

Bang!

The exterior door behind her flew open with a loud smack. Ruby spun around, immediately on alert, as a man and a woman exploded into the room. The woman was impossibly tall, well over six feet, gripping a Glock in both hands. The man was short, but heavy with muscle.

Walters must have known Ruby would show up at the bus station—or at least thought it was a possibility—and he'd sent these two assailants here to ambush her.

All of this flashed through her mind in a millisecond. Meanwhile, her instincts had her dropping into a fighting stance, scanning the small space for anything she could use as a weapon.

An arm's length away, the woman took aim. Was she really going to fire shots inside a bus station restroom, where someone would hear and come investigate? Was Walters that desperate?

As if in response, she barked at her partner, "Get her outside, now!"

The man grabbed Ruby roughly by the waist and yanked her out the open door. Ruby resisted with every muscle in her body, adrenaline overruling the pain of her injuries, but his strength was overwhelming. In the space of an instant, she was dragged into the overflow parking lot behind the station.

"The door!" the woman yelled. "Or people will hear!"

He kicked the door shut behind them while his partner followed closely with her Glock. Ruby craned her head to see behind her, and her stomach rolled over. They were forcing her into a densely wooded area behind the parking lot… where there would be no witnesses.

Ruby couldn't let that happen.

Her hand shot out, lightning-fast, and smacked the Glock from the woman's grip. Somewhere on the edges of her consciousness, Ruby was aware of pain exploding from her left side, but it was drowned by her adrenaline.

Fight first, freak out later.

Ruby went limp in the man's arms, making him temporarily lose his hold. She ducked under his arm, spun around and kicked out the backs of his knees. He dropped like a load of bricks, writhing in pain.

The woman dove to the ground and retrieved her gun, but Ruby slammed her hand against the pavement. She yelped in pain but held fast to her grip. She pushed back hard, sending Ruby stumbling backward. Before she could regain her balance, the woman cupped the back of her head and shoved it toward a utility pole. If Ruby's head hit that punishing surface, it would mean lights out. These attackers would drag her into those woods, put a bullet in her, and she'd never wake up again.

Her instincts taking over, Ruby jerked to the side, barely grazing the pole with the side of her cheek. Pain still exploded through her face, but her mind stayed clear. She dropped into a roll and popped back up behind the woman. Using the force of her own momentum, she sent her fist crashing into the woman's hand. The Glock dropped to the ground.

Violence sickened Ruby's stomach. She'd joined the Bureau to deliver justice, not pain and injury. But she was under attack, and she needed to fight back with all her strength if she was going to survive.

Lord, please deliver me. Please don't let this end in death for anyone.

Ruby scraped the Glock off the pavement, but before she could make another move, her injured arm was twisted painfully behind her back.

The thickly muscled man had recovered and was pinning Ruby against him.

"Drop the gun! On your knees, now!"

Pain burned through her, so intense she nearly blacked out. Tears gathered in her eyes and she struggled to breathe against an agony so fierce it filled every pocket of her mind.

Focus, Ruby. Fight past the pain.

Slowly, she lowered the gun to the ground, and he snatched it up and tucked it into his waistband. With sheer will, Ruby dragged herself from the edge of unconsciousness and forced her vision to clear. She turned to look at her captor, and the blood froze in her veins when she saw what he held in his hand.

A syringe.

So, that was the plan. Inject her with a knockout drug, drag her into the woods, and put a bullet into her.

She could *not* allow these people to put that syringe in her arm. She'd never wake up.

"On your knees!" the man snarled.

Slowly, Ruby obeyed, her mind racing. The man had to bend forward to maintain Ruby's arm pinned behind her back, and the Glock he'd tucked into his waistband was only inches away.

His partner had recovered and planted herself in front of Ruby, snarling with anger. Apparently, she hadn't appreciated the punch to the hand. A hunger for revenge gleamed in her eyes, and she cocked back her arm, aiming for Ruby's face.

Ruby dodged at the last second, and the blow struck the man's leg instead. He bellowed in frustration more than pain and took out his anger on Ruby's arm, jerking it back harder. Fresh pain streaked through the injured joint and she nearly passed out again.

"Enough!" he shouted. "We don't have time for that! Help me drag her into the woods."

Ruby's heart locked up tight like a vise. Her left arm was incapacitated and she was on her knees; this man could sink that needle into her at any moment. Her only hope was the Glock tucked inches away at his waist, and she needed to reach for it, no matter the consequences.

It was time to act.

Quick as a flash, she slid the weapon from the man's waistband and fired a shot straight into the woman's leg.

Then time slowed, and everything happened at once.

The woman crumpled onto the pavement. The man let out a sharp cry of disbelief. A sharp burn pierced Ruby's skin as the needle sank into her arm.

Cold dread dropped into her gut like a ball of ice. She needed to overpower her attackers and get away before the drug took effect—but a high dose administered by injection could cause a swift loss of consciousness. She had to act fast.

Lord, give me Your strength.

Fueled by desperation, strengthened by her Father, Ruby shot to her feet before the other two could react. She spun around, placing herself behind the man, and struck him across the back of his skull with the Glock, praying the blow wasn't hard enough to cause permanent damage. He dropped hard on the cement, unconscious.

The woman gritted her teeth as she slowly rose, blood pulsing from her leg, and limped toward Ruby. A hard glint of determination shone in her eyes. She wouldn't give up without a fight.

Neither would Ruby.

Using her speed and compact size to her advantage, Ruby crouched low, spun to gain momentum and landed a vicious roundhouse kick straight to the taller woman's ribs. The crack of fissured bone split the air, and the woman shrieked and doubled over in pain. Ruby didn't allow her a chance to recover. She gripped her neck in one hand with the intention of shoving her into the pavement, but she twisted away at the last minute. She reached for the gun Ruby still held in her right hand—a sloppy move that Ruby should have easily avoided, but her head was starting to feel fuzzy. The woman managed to knock it out of her hand, and it clanged against the concrete.

A heavy, sleepy feeling teased the edge of Ruby's brain, but she resisted its pull. She couldn't give in yet. She needed to finish this first and somehow escape.

The woman's lip curled up in a smirk. "Feeling that shot yet, Isadora?"

No, she wasn't Isadora. She was— Who was she again?

Fluffy clouds of oblivion filled her brain and muddled her vision.

No! Not yet.

The woman cocked back to punch her, but she dodged at the last second, and the woman stumbled forward on her own momentum.

This was Ruby's last chance. She needed to deal a final blow now—while her opponent was off-balance.

And before she succumbed to this heavy, insistent pull of sleep.

Ruby reached for the gun that had skittered across the pavement, teetering as her world tilted. She lost her footing, splayed across the ground, but managed to close her hand around the Glock. She'd gripped this type of weapon so many times, she didn't need to think. Instincts kicked in.

She rolled onto her back, lifted the gun and fired a shot into the woman's shoulder. She gasped, gripping her injury, and collapsed.

Ruby glanced at her other attacker, who was still out cold but could wake up at any moment. She needed to get out of there—fast.

Trouble was, her brain was grinding to a halt, taking her body with it.

She squinted into the distance, her vision black around the edges. A big, gray bus was pulling out onto the road. The bus she was supposed to be on.

Her heart sank with despair. She was going to pass out beside her attackers, and they would wake up and find her there. And then…

Cold fear flashed through her. There would be no trial. No justice.

An idea pierced the fog of her mind. Could she make it to Dex's truck? It was so far away, and her legs were so heavy…

And the keys were locked inside it.

Still, she needed to move. To put some distance between herself and these assailants. With supreme effort, she stood and put one foot in front of the other. Why did her left foot hurt so much? She'd done something to it, but she couldn't remember what.

Her body was so, so heavy, she was shuffling. The bus station beside her was spinning. The blackness edging her vision was spreading, blotting out the world.

Sensing her balance failing, she threw out her hands and felt cold cement beneath her palms. The space around her was narrower. She was in the alley beside the station, one last lucid corner of her brain told her.

The door to the station was only a few feet away. She wasn't going to make it. She banged her hip into something and winced. A dumpster. It threw off what little remained of her balance and she tumbled to the ground, no longer aware of anything but the rotting smell of garbage and the blinding pain radiating through her body.

Lord, I hurt so much. Lord—

The world around her went dark.

Dex's heart *stopped.*

I borrowed your truck to drive to the bus station. The keys are locked inside. I'm sorry.

He shot out of his chair stationed near Ruby's door and burst into her bedroom.

Of course it was empty.

Panic raced up his spine. She'd taken off in the middle of the night, injured and alone, with murderers hunting her.

She'd eliminated his ability to protect her.

He understood why she'd done it, though that didn't make it any less reckless. She was sacrificing herself to protect him and Oliver, a noble and infuriating gesture that made his entire body simmer with rage and sharp, ice-cold fear.

Dex ran to the bunkhouse and shook Nate awake.

"I need to go handle something," he said to the bleary-eyed ranch hand. Nancy wasn't scheduled to arrive for another hour, and he couldn't leave his eight-year-old nephew alone. "Keep an eye on Oliver until I get back."

Without further explanation, Dex grabbed his spare keys from the lodge and jumped into his other pickup. His mind raced as he flew down the highway toward the bus station. Would he get there in time, or was Ruby already on a bus headed far away from him?

Or had her attackers caught up with her?

He wouldn't leave her to face them alone. The pounding of his heart and the twist in his gut screamed at him to get to her. *Now.*

He used Bluetooth to call her number, but after a few rings it went to voicemail. Desperate, he dialed Reyes and explained the situation.

"I'll meet you at the station with a couple of deputies," the sheriff told him. "Any idea when she left?"

Guilt crashed into him like a wrecking ball. He'd promised to take care of her, and he'd failed.

"No," he admitted, his voice thick with regret. He'd stayed awake, guarding her door, so she must have slipped out the window at some point in the night. He hadn't anticipated that, and now she was alone and in danger. "I think the first bus of the day leaves at 6:00 a.m." He checked the digital display on his dash. A few minutes ago—and he was still fifteen minutes from the station. He wanted to pound the steering wheel with frustration, but a temper tantrum wouldn't help Ruby.

"I'll call the bus station," Reyes said. "I'll give them her description and tell them to not allow her on the bus if it hasn't left yet."

A spark of hope shot through Dex. "Great idea. Thanks."

He knew he could rely on Reyes. Since Dex had moved back to the ranch after his military service, he and Reyes had gotten pretty tight. Especially after the sheriff's wife had been tragically killed a couple of years ago.

"I'll be there in ten minutes." It would have been closer to fifteen if Dex was doing the legal limit—which he definitely *wasn't* doing.

"I'll be right behind you." Reyes ended the call.

Dex pushed his pickup to the max, the needle on the speedometer trembling at the edge of its limit. Luckily, there weren't many cars on the road at this time of the morning, and he arrived in nine minutes.

He swerved into the bus station, pulling to a screeching stop crosswise over two parking spots. His other truck was right there in the lot, just as Ruby had indicated. His gaze traveled over the fleet of buses parked behind the station, none idling or boarding passengers.

Lord, please don't let me be too late.

He leapt out of the truck, his hand hovering instinctively over the gun at his hip. He burst through the station doors, causing the woman behind the counter to shrink back.

"Have you seen a young woman, dark hair—"

"Yes," the employee cut in, her voice high with fear. "The sheriff called about her."

"Where is she?" Dex demanded, too revved up to be polite.

"Sh...she bought her ticket a while ago, then went to the

ladies' room," the woman stuttered, obviously shaken. "She hasn't come out. The bus left without her."

Fear exploded through Dex's veins. He raced to the women's restroom and banged on the door. The woman behind the counter followed him.

"I already tried knocking. She locked the door, and she isn't responding."

Dex's heart pounded like a piston. Why wasn't she answering? Was she hurt? "Was she in there alone?" he barked at the poor bus station employee.

She blinked her wide eyes. "I… I think so. I was busy checking people in, so I—"

Dex was no longer listening. He stepped back and slammed his boot flat into the wooden door just below the lock. The door burst open with a bang.

The restroom was empty.

Dex checked the only stall, just in case, icy fingers of panic snaking up his spine. No one was in there. He dialed her number again, and was surprised to hear a soft buzzing…

Emanating from the wastebasket.

He picked away a few used paper towels from the bin to reveal the glowing screen of Ruby's phone.

So she'd been in here. She'd sent that final text to him and tossed her phone in the garbage. She'd feared her enemies were tracking her, so she'd left it behind.

But she hadn't boarded that bus, she hadn't returned to the waiting area, and she hadn't taken off in his truck. Desperation consumed him, his mind racing.

Where in the world had she *gone*?

His gaze landed on an exterior door that opened to the back parking lot. Could she have escaped that way?

Twisting the door handle, Dex pushed his way outside. No one was there; just a handful of parked cars. A wooded area lined the back, and the worst possible images flooded Dex's imagination. *God, please, don't let Ruby's enemies have dragged her back there.* His stomach sank, his mind tormented with what she might be enduring right now.

Or if she was still alive.

No, he couldn't think that way. It would destroy him.

Hushed voices reached his ears. A man and a woman. It sounded like they were in the alley beside the bus station. Neither voice was Ruby's, but Dex's instincts crackled and he broke into a run.

The voices rose and sharpened in fear, then footsteps pounded the pavement—like whoever was in that alley had heard him coming and was running away.

Dex accelerated to a sprint, hitting the alley just as a car peeled out of the lot. He was going to jump back into his truck and chase it down when he nearly tripped over a small, crumpled form slumped against the dumpster. He looked down and all the air escaped his lungs. He sank to his knees.

Ruby.

Dear Lord... Let her be alive. Please.

He gathered her into his arms, and her head lolled onto his shoulder. Dread knifing his gut, he pressed two fingers to the side of her neck.

There was a pulse. It was slow, but strong. *Father, thank You.* He scanned her beautiful face, her left cheek swollen, the beginnings of a violet bruise spreading over her eye. A wave of frustration and helplessness crashed over him, drowning him. Why had she run off? Why wouldn't she accept his help? Who was hurting her?

At this last thought, his emotions morphed into simmering rage. Whoever was after Ruby wasn't just facing one tiny woman all alone. They had Dex to contend with, along with the entire Cooper County Sheriff's Department.

Dex was going to hunt down those cowards and make them face justice.

Police sirens sliced the air, announcing the arrival of Reyes and his deputies. Dex lifted Ruby easily, though the fact that she was deadweight in his arms worried him deeply. If she'd been knocked unconscious, she would have at least stirred when he'd lifted her. But she was acting as if she'd been drugged.

He stepped out of the alleyway to find Reyes charging toward him.

"What happened?"

Dex didn't break stride as he carried his precious cargo to his truck. "I found her like this in the alley."

Reyes's eyebrows shot up as he looked Ruby over. "She looks like she's been drugged."

Dex opened his truck with one hand, curling Ruby into his chest with the other. "When I got here, a man and a woman were in that alley with her. They took off in their car when they heard me coming, before I could get a look at them."

Reyes called over one of his deputies. "You get the plates?"

Dex rattled off the letters and numbers. Reyes looked grateful but not surprised. They both had combat experience, and they'd both learned to pay attention to details, even in high-stress situations.

"Call in those plates," Reyes told his deputy. "And get an ambulance over here, quick. We've got to transport the victim to the hospital—"

"I can get her there faster." Dex gently slid Ruby into his passenger seat and closed the door. He jogged around to the driver's side and hopped in, not waiting for Reyes to protest.

The lawman didn't even try. "I'll call ahead for you, let them know you're coming." He settled a sober gaze on his friend. "Keep me updated. And I'll let you know what we find here at the crime scene."

Gratitude swelled in Dex's chest, but he just nodded and pulled out of the lot. He wasn't wasting any time when it came to Ruby's well-being. He would deal with cops and questions later.

He exceeded every speed limit, clocking a record time to Butte Valley Regional Hospital. Staff was already there, waiting by the curb with a gurney.

Dex felt powerless as hospital staff took over, shooing him away as they whisked Ruby through automatic doors. He watched her small form disappear, his heart tightening. A hospital employee invited him to sit and wait, but he was too restless. He paced the waiting room, his mind flying in a hundred different directions. Ruby had snuck away to protect him and Oliver. What dangerous people were after her, and why? Dex couldn't believe she was involved in anything criminal. She was secretive, sure. She was wary and kept to herself. But she was so genuinely kind. So sincere when she interacted with him and everyone else at the ranch.

Unless all of it was a lie.

Those bottomless dark eyes tended to muddle his logic.

A hospital staffer handed him a clipboard full of forms. He answered the questions he could, leaving everything else blank. Who, really, was Ruby Laurier? She hadn't provided any emergency contacts on her job application. Did she have any family? Anyone he should be contacting right now? He wouldn't know until he talked to her, *if* she would even answer his questions.

While he waited, he dialed Nate's cell to check on Oliver.

His young ranch hand picked up on the first ring. "Hey, Dex."

Dex's pulse kicked up even higher. This wasn't Nate's

typical, easygoing tone. This was a something-is-definitely-wrong tone.

"Everything okay?"

A sigh came over the line. "Oliver's just fine, playing trains in his room. But Nancy called..."

Impatient, Dex gripped the phone tighter. "And?"

"She's, ah, not coming."

A wave of weariness washed over him. He didn't need this headache right now. "Why? Is she not feeling well?"

Pause. "She was pretty spooked after yesterday."

Dex had to admit he wasn't entirely surprised. He'd tried to smooth over the incident the previous night, but she'd fled the ranch like she was under enemy attack.

"Did she say when she would come back?"

Nate cleared his throat, and Dex suspected he wasn't going to like his answer. "She, ah, said she wouldn't come back until Ruby was gone. Said 'that girl is trouble.'"

Dex balled his fist, anger flooding him, and opened his mouth to defend Ruby, to insist that she wasn't "trouble," but his own logic contradicted him. She had, in fact, brought her problems with her to his ranch. Her presence placed them all in danger, including Oliver, and he could hardly blame Nancy for wanting none of it. She'd signed up to nanny a little boy, not dodge bullets. If Dex had any sense, he'd tell Ruby to pack up her troubles and take them elsewhere.

And yet, his heart would not allow him to abandon this spirited and vulnerable woman. The drive to protect her was so strong he felt it must have been placed there by the Lord. That meant he would have to figure out how to protect his young nephew *and* his mysterious employee.

"Well, Nate, you've officially been promoted from ranch hand to nanny, at least until I figure something else out."

Nate laughed. "You've got it, boss."

Nate was a good kid, and as the oldest of many siblings, more than qualified for the job. "And the promotion comes with a raise, too." Dex looked up to see a nurse headed his way.

"Mr. Dexler? Come with me, please."

"Gotta go for now," he told Nate. "Keep an eye on my kiddo until I get back."

He hung up and followed the nurse back to Ruby's room. When he walked in the door, his heart stuttered painfully. She'd always seemed so tough, a little pistol who roped cattle, rode hard, and didn't take any lip from anyone.

Now, sleeping in this hospital bed with machines beeping all around her, she looked so small and vulnerable. Worry knotted Dex's stomach, and he wished she'd sit up and argue with him already.

He swallowed down the knot of emotion choking him. "Is she…going to be okay?"

The nurse gave him a reassuring smile. "Absolutely. Blood tests revealed high levels of Midazolam in her system, which is why she's unconscious. It's not enough to cause any permanent damage, though, and all her vitals are good."

Dex had suspected she'd been drugged, but it was chilling to hear the confirmation. Someone had incapacitated her with the intention of dragging her off somewhere.

The nurse, all business, asked no questions as to the whys and hows. That was the cops' job. She and the rest of the medical team were making Ruby well. That was their priority.

"Feel free to sit with her if you like," the nurse said. "We expect her to wake up shortly, though she'll be sleepy for a while."

"Thank you."

The nurse left, and Dex pulled a chair close to Ruby's bed, needing to be near her.

He leaned forward and brushed a dark, silky curl from her cheek. The bruise he'd noticed earlier had darkened to an angry purple, and rage seared through his veins.

"I won't let anyone hurt you again," he said, his voice rough with emotion. It was pointless talking to her when she wasn't even conscious, but he wouldn't have had the nerve to show his emotion with those dark, penetrating eyes glaring back at him. He swept his gaze over her pixie face. "You're going to be all right, Killer. You're a fighter. If you've got a bruise like that, I don't wanna see how banged up the other guys are."

She shifted in her bed and let out a faint murmur, like she'd heard him. Her eyes fluttered, those long, dark eyelashes fanning over the tops of her cheeks.

"Dex?"

Emotion slammed into him with the force of a tidal wave. She wasn't fully awake yet, but she was asking for him. When he responded, his voice came out gravelly.

"I'm right here, Ruby."

She didn't respond, and as the seconds ticked by, Dex's tension mounted. Was she awake? Dreaming?

"Are you in pain?"

She mumbled something, like her mouth wasn't quite working yet, but she didn't sound uncomfortable.

"I…sorry."

Her voice was all mumbly and garbled, and it made Dex's heart ache. "We can talk when you're ready. Rest now."

She quieted, but her fingers twitched like she was reaching for him. "Dex."

It was too much. He melted on the spot. "Would you like me to hold your hand?"

"Mmm."

He wrapped his hand around hers, loving the feel of her soft skin. Loving how her hand fit so well inside his. "It's okay, Ruby. You can sleep. I'm not going anywhere."

She did just that for the next hour. Dex messaged Nate to check on Oliver and the ranch. Everything was fine with Nate at the helm, and when Dex looked up from his phone, a set of captivating dark eyes were settled on him.

Dex stared back for a moment, lost in that gaze and unsure what to say. He was relieved. He was angry. He was frustrated and confused and a jumble of other things he couldn't even untangle.

"I'm sorry I ran off." Ruby's voice shook, like she was about to cry.

Dex's anger melted away. He never could bear a woman's tears, especially not from this particular woman who had his heart wrapped around her pinkie. "You were trying to protect Oliver and me from whoever's after you."

"Yes." Her eyes shone with tears that she was too stubborn to let fall.

His fingers were still threaded through hers, and he made no move to let go. "You didn't need to do that, Ruby. I know you're scared—too scared to even tell me who these people are—but you don't need to face all this alone." He dragged in a deep breath and brushed his thumb over her knuckles. "I can keep you safe."

She squeezed her eyes shut, like she was battling herself. Even with her swollen, purple cheek and tear-filled eyes, she was the bravest, strongest, most beautiful woman Dex had ever met.

When she opened her eyes, they shone with an intense determination. "Dex, you've been so good to me. Better than I deserve. I owe you the truth, and I'm going to give it to you."

His pulse quickened and he leaned in closer. "Tell me, Ruby. Tell me what I need to know to help you."

She sucked in a ragged breath, and when she looked up at him, fear flashed in her eyes. "Dex, I'm not who you think I am."

FIVE

Ruby knew there was no point in lying anymore. She'd tried to disappear and lead Walters away from Dex's ranch, but the ruthless senator had them on his radar now. She'd failed them; now the least she could do was let Dex know what he was facing.

And on an emotional level, she couldn't bear to deceive Dex any longer. Her heart was sick with all the lies, and she needed to come clean to cleanse her soul.

But would Dex forgive her for the last four months of deception?

She inhaled a cautious breath, bracing herself for his anger. "Dex, I was placed at your ranch four months ago as part of the Witness Protection Program."

His expression went slack with disbelief, but she pressed on, needing to unburden herself before she lost her nerve.

"In six days, I'm set to testify in a high-profile case against a very dangerous person. That person caught up with me yesterday."

The shock on his face sharpened to anger. Betrayal flashed in his eyes, and Ruby's gut twisted into a tight knot. She had a feeling he wouldn't be handing out forgiveness anytime soon. Maybe ever.

A long moment ticked by in silence, her staring into the storm raging in his eyes, awaiting his response.

"So, this whole time…" His voice shook with emotion. "You've been lying to me?"

Her heart slammed into her rib cage. "I couldn't blow my cover. I didn't have a choice—"

"You had the choice to trust me." The anger in his eyes melted into a deep well of hurt. "You could have let me help you instead of pushing me away."

Her heart was fissuring, but she continued, trying to make him understand. "I was trying to protect you and Oliver. I'm sorry I dragged you into all this. I'm sorry you're now in danger because of me. I'm…so sorry."

Her voice broke, and Dex's expression softened a little, but he looked away. "So your name's not really Ruby Laurier, is it?"

She looked down, twisting her blanket in her hand. "No."

"And let me guess, you can't tell me who you really are?"

Despair ballooned inside her chest, choking her. "Dex, I wish I could, but—"

"And I suppose you won't tell me the identity of this dangerous, high-profile person who's after you?"

She covered her face with her hands. "Dex, I'm sorry. You know I can't."

He looked away, the muscle in his jaw flexing. "Why am I not surprised? You've deceived me since I first met you. Why would that change now?"

"That's not fair!" She twisted the blanket tighter in her fist, her frustration mounting. "I'm in the WITSEC program. I couldn't blow my cover."

He started pacing the small room. "Speaking of which, the US marshals are charged with the protection of WITSEC witnesses. Why haven't you called them?"

"I did. Then a carload of thugs with guns showed up."

Dex stopped short and whirled on her, his expression a mask of shock. "The attackers in the SUV yesterday?"

She nodded.

He pushed a fist through his hair. It was shiny and dark and a touch too long for an ex-military guy. "Are you saying the US Marshals Service is compromised?"

She shrugged. "I made contact using the established protocols. Then scary dudes showed up trying to kill me. The marshals never arrived as promised, and they never contacted me."

Dex's eyes widened, and he dropped back into his chair. "That means…"

"I'm on my own." Ruby's heart squeezed, but she wrestled back her despair.

The muscle in Dex's jaw flexed. "How did you get mixed up in something like this? You're obviously not some average victim or eyewitness. You fight like a professional."

She hated the suspicion in his eyes. Did he think she was involved in organized or federal-level crime, talking to the feds for a plea deal? She longed to tell him her real background, but that would mean divulging details of a very sensitive, very high-profile case.

She swallowed hard. "Dex, I hope you believe me when I say I'm not involved in anything illegal."

He raked a glacial gaze over her, then let out his breath. "I know."

"You do?"

He rubbed his chin, pensive. "With your training, I'm guessing military or law enforcement. Either way, you're not the criminal type. I just…know."

She released a breath of relief. At least he didn't think the worst of her.

"Look, Ruby—" He ran a hand down his face. "I understand you thought you had no choice. I just…don't like when people lie to me." His irises flickered like blue flames. "It's hard for me to trust them again."

A heavy, icy ball sank into her gut. Dex would never see her the same way again.

But she was an agent for the Federal Bureau of Investigation, following protocol. Dex's opinion was secondary to her mission.

Even though the ache in her heart suggested otherwise.

She sat up taller, trying to regain her composure. "Look, I won't tangle you up in this any longer. Once I'm discharged, I'll disappear."

His posture went rigid. "No."

"No?" She bristled at his authoritative tone.

He looked down, and a shiny lock of hair fell over his eyes. "You're smart and you're tough, Ruby. You really are." He stood and paced again, his body taut as a bow. "But whoever this person is—" He frowned, obviously frustrated by his lack of information. "He's able to track you wherever you go. Going alone is asking for trouble."

Ruby's heart pinched painfully. He still wanted to help her? Even though she'd hurt him and destroyed his trust?

She gripped the hospital blanket tighter. "If I go back to the ranch, these guys will show up again."

"I know," he conceded, his voice tinged with frustration. He stopped his pacing and dragged his fingers through his hair. "I know."

"So, you see that I have no choice—"

"You do have a choice." He finally snapped his gaze back to her, his eyes igniting.

"What choice?"

He strode over to the bed, planted his palms against the

foot of the mattress and leaned over her. "Let me protect you. With the help of Reyes and the sheriff's department."

Ruby's gut cramped with fear, and she drilled her eyes into his. "No cops." She couldn't trust them. She couldn't trust anyone right now. Except maybe Dex, but she wouldn't place this burden on him.

Dex's handsome features darkened with frustration. "Ruby—"

"I'm..." *I'm injured and unarmed and vulnerable...* "I'm fine on my own."

His pale blue irises flashed as he leaned over her. "You're not. Your pulse is racing at the base of your throat, and your every muscle is tense. You're hurt and terrified and too proud to let anyone help you."

She wasn't about to admit he was right. She closed her eyes and bit the inside of her cheek, determined to hold back her tears.

"Look, Reyes and I have known each other for a long time. He's...been through a lot. Things he doesn't like to talk about, but the point is this—he's a good cop and a good person and I trust him. Which means you can, too."

Ruby twisted her blanket in her hands, wavering.

"Plus, he offered to keep deputies patrolling the ranch around the clock."

She blinked her eyes open. "He offered to do that?"

Dex's gaze burned into hers a moment longer before he looked away again. "He wants to catch these guys, too. I think it's a safe bet they'll return."

A chill traced up her spine. "Which is why I shouldn't go back."

"Look, Ruby." Dex rounded the bed until he was standing beside her, his jaw tight and his posture rigid. "I...appreciate that you're trying to protect Oliver and me." His mouth turned down, and Ruby read the subtext: *Even though I don't appreciate the lies.* He cleared his throat. "But with deputies patrolling the place, and you and I staying vigilant, we'll catch whoever is tracking you. But if you run off on your own…" He stuffed his fists into his pockets, like he was pushing down a strong emotion. "It won't end well."

Lord, he cares about me. He genuinely did; Ruby could see it on his face. After all her lies, he still wanted to protect her. But would he ever forgive her? Would things ever be the same between them?

In a few days, it wouldn't matter, she reminded herself. She would testify then return to her life in DC.

What life? asked a nasty little voice in her head. She shook off the self-inflicted barb. She didn't have the bandwidth for soul-searching right now.

She looked down at her thin hospital blanket, wrinkled and misshapen from twisting it in her hands. "You're sacrificing too much for me. You…don't have to do this."

His expression darkened and he looked away. "I'll go talk to Reyes. We'll plan a rotation for his officers."

Dex started for the door, and Ruby stared sadly at his retreating back. He was so *angry* with her. So hurt. She'd destroyed her relationship with the one person in her life who cared about her. And yet here he was, staying with her at the hospital, organizing her security, opening his home to her.

Just before he walked out the door, he turned. He must have noticed the sadness in her eyes, because he sighed heavily and his expression melted…a little. "Look, uh, get some rest, okay?" He drummed his fingers restlessly against the doorframe. "We'll sort this out."

Ruby opened her mouth to say…she wasn't sure what. *Thank you for trying to keep me alive? I'm sorry I lied to you for the last four months?* No words felt right, and they died on her lips. It didn't matter anyway.

Dex had already walked out the door.

Dex peeked his head inside Ruby's room at 8:00 a.m. to find her still asleep. He'd brought her home from the hospital yesterday afternoon, and she'd spent the remainder of the day dozing, sleeping off the effects of the drugs in her system.

She was still sleeping hard, her small fists curled around her blanket, heartbreakingly vulnerable. Her thick, glossy hair fanned over her pillow, wild and rebellious, just like her, and those long, dark eyelashes brushed the tops of her cheeks.

She was so exquisitely beautiful, it hurt to look at her.

Meanwhile, his logic waged battle with the emotions battering his soul.

She lied to me.

But she had to.

She hid her identity from me.

But she let me see who she really is, on the inside.

God, why did You place Ruby in my life, so she could betray me?

It wasn't an accusation, but a sincere question. Why was it God's plan that he fall for this pint-sized fireball—and being honest, he'd fallen hard—only to have her rip his heart to shreds?

Just like his ex, who had hidden her drug addiction from him for months, manipulating him into giving her large sums of money to fund it. When he'd pieced together the truth, the shock had rocked him, throwing his world off its axis. He'd encouraged her to seek help, but when she'd realized he wouldn't be bankrolling her next high, she'd disappeared from his life. Even now, fresh feelings of betrayal washed over him in a tide of bitter cold. Since that abrupt rupture with the only woman he'd ever loved, he'd been incapable of trust.

But he didn't want to dwell on that. He shoved the past hurts from his mind, straightened his spine and stepped out of the room. If it was God's plan that he protect Ruby as she walked this treacherous path, he could do that. But he would keep his distance emotionally. Because even if he managed to forgive her, could he ever trust her again? She'd ripped the bandage off his old wounds and left him bleeding.

At the sound of a car pulling into the driveway, Dex glanced out the window. Sheriff Reyes. The next pair of deputies was arriving to relieve the overnight shift.

When Oliver had woken up this morning, he'd peppered Dex with questions about the police presence. Thus far, Dex had managed to downplay the situation, telling him his buddy, Sheriff Reyes, was keeping an eye on things around the ranch and there was nothing to worry about. Then Dex had offered to make him pancakes, and the eight-year-old had been thoroughly appeased.

Not for the first time, Dex worried that Ruby's presence was endangering his young nephew. Yet, every time the thought crossed his mind, a feeling of peace—a feeling of rightness—filled his soul. The Lord was telling him to keep Ruby close and that their safety was in His hands.

Dex grabbed a mug from the cupboard and filled it with coffee that had just finished auto-brewing. He stepped out onto the porch and headed for Reyes's cruiser.

The sheriff emerged from the car, along with a couple of his deputies. "How was your night?"

Dex took a sip from his cup, the hot liquid warming him. "No news, so good news. Want a coffee?"

Reyes shook his head. "Nah, had some back at the office. How's your patient?"

Dex frowned. "She's pretty banged up."

"I imagine that between the pain meds and the residual effects of the knockout drug, she's been sleeping a lot."

Dex thought of her fingers curled around her blanket, tucked away safe in his lodge.

He shoved the thought aside and cleared his throat. "Yeah, and she's gonna wake up cranky."

"You're right about that."

Not Reyes's voice, but Ruby's. Dex turned to find her standing on the porch, barefoot, pajama-clad, with her hair a messy lion's mane around her head.

He'd never seen a more beautiful woman in his life, and it tore him to shreds.

"You feeling sore?" he asked softly.

"Only in about three-quarters of my body."

His lips tipped up. "A coffee and some painkillers sound good?"

She tilted her head to the side. "Just a coffee. I'll go grab it."

She turned to head back inside, but Dex was faster. "I'll get it for you. And there's no need to be a tough guy about the painkillers. You'll be more comfortable if you take them."

She officially had two cracked ribs, a badly bruised shoulder, a light sprain in her left ankle and a mild concussion. The hospital had prescribed pain medication when they'd discharged her.

She shook her head and winced. "I need my mind clear," she said under her breath so only Dex could hear. For some reason, she was wary of everyone but him, even though he'd assured her Reyes could be trusted.

But if Ruby was only going to feel safe with one man, Dex wanted it to be him.

"Ruby, you're in pain. Stop being stubborn and take the medicine the doctor prescribed you."

Her hands shot to her hips. "Have I mentioned how bossy you are?"

Dex opened his mouth to defend himself, but Reyes let out a hoot of laughter. "Well, I'll let you-all sort this out without an audience." The two overnight deputies had joined them, as well as their replacements. "We'll take a stroll around the perimeter while my officers debrief."

Ruby lifted a brow at Dex and waved at the deputies. "Thanks, guys!" she called out, then stomped back inside.

Dex followed, his frustration simmering. "Sit down." He gestured to the soft chairs in the living room. "I'll bring you a coffee."

He expected her to protest, because that was her MO, but she instead collapsed into a chair and laid her head back. Dex's protectiveness flared as he poured coffee into a mug and added a splash of milk, which was how she liked it.

Yeah, he'd noticed.

He crossed the room, and she reached for the steaming mug.

"Thank you." She took a careful sip.

"For being pushy?" He perched on the ottoman at her feet. "You're welcome."

She grinned, wincing a little, and he huffed out an impatient sigh.

"At least let me give you some over-the-counter stuff."

"I already raided your medicine cabinet. Hope you don't mind."

He didn't mind at all. In fact, his irrational heart throbbed at the thought of her padding barefoot into his master bath, making herself right at home. It made him dream of things he had no right to.

Dex shook off the inconvenient thoughts. "How'd you sleep?"

Her grin died on her lips. "Better than I should have, considering people are trying to kill me."

He sighed. "Which is why you're refusing meds."

She raised her cup in mock salute. "Or maybe I'm just trying to drive you nuts."

"Not trying. Succeeding."

He longed for her to feel utterly safe with him. Safe enough to slumber away into oblivion, trusting he would protect her. The primal part of him needed that deep level of trust from her. The rational part of him recognized that he would be just as vigilant if killers were after *him*.

But he'd given up on logic when it came to Ruby. With her, he just felt. He just *needed.*

Man, was he in trouble.

She tossed him an impish look. "So, boss, what's the plan?"

Always so insolent.

He really shouldn't love it.

He scowled at her, but her answering grin told him she didn't believe it for a second. He pushed up onto his feet and paced the room. "The plan is that you're going to stay inside, out of sight and resting."

Her expression turned petulant. "Sounds boring."

He stopped in his tracks and whirled on her. "It sounds *necessary.* These people who are after you—whose identities you won't divulge—are just waiting to get their hands on you. The last thing I need is you wandering off."

She frowned. "You make me sound like a naughty child."

"You climbed out a window last night and stole my truck!"

She flipped her hair over her shoulder. "I borrowed your truck."

He dragged a hand down his face. This woman was going to kill him. "Ruby, just stay inside."

She lifted her chin and met his eye. "Not happening. I can help you and the sheriffs protect the property."

He threw up his hands. "If you're milling around this ranch, you're only making the job of protecting you harder!"

She shrugged. "Agree to disagree."

"No, I will not!" He barreled into the kitchen and slammed his half-empty coffee mug into the sink.

"Stop throwing a tantrum." Ruby's voice was exasperatingly calm.

He spun around to face her. "I'm not tantruming! I'm tidying up."

She crossed her arms over her chest, not buying it. "Whatever you say. Look, I think we can compromise here."

He arched a brow. "Is that so? What do you propose?"

She slowly set her mug on the end table beside her, suddenly tense. "Look, I'm sorry I hid it from you before, but you've probably figured out by now that I'm a really good shot."

All those months of her refusing to use a gun. Dex had thought she was squeamish about firearms, but now he understood it was just a cover. Fresh feelings of betrayal flooded him, and he looked away.

"I really am sorry that I kept all of this from you," she said softly, the teasing tone absent from her voice. "Knowing you now, I realize I could have trusted you."

He met her eyes, saw a well of genuine regret, and a bit of the weight lifted from his chest. *Knowing you now, I realize I could have trusted you.*

She'd shown up four months ago, alone and afraid, wary of everyone she met. Could he really blame her?

Torn between anger and the need to forgive, he set aside the thought for later. "So what exactly are you suggesting?"

"You give me a Glock, and I patrol the perimeter of the lodge."

He bristled. "You know, you don't need to do that. The deputies and I have this under control."

"I…know." She pushed a hand through her tangle of curls, looking sweet and vulnerable all of a sudden. Dex took a step toward her before he could stop himself. "The drugs weren't the only reason I slept so well last night."

Dex's resolve melted. He closed the space between them, his arms tingling to wrap around her. He looked deeply into her eyes. "Then let me protect you."

"I am." Her eyes flashed with an emotion he would be dreaming about that night. "But I want to help. I need to help. I can't just sit inside this lodge like a porcelain doll in a glass case."

Dex exhaled a frustrated breath, slowly pushing it out through clenched teeth. His protectiveness was clashing with her need for independence. He wanted her as far from this threat as possible, but she needed to feel strong.

He got that.

"The Glock is yours."

She settled an insistent look on him. "And the perimeter?"

His shoulders tensed as tight as a piano string. "How wide of a perimeter?"

"An arm's length from the lodge at all times."

He growled. "And you'll take breaks to rest?"

"*Lots* of breaks. To rest and hang out with Oliver."

He ran a dubious gaze over her beautiful face. "If I suffer a heart attack, it'll be on your conscience."

She lifted a brow. "Is that a yes?"

He blew out a gusty breath of defeat. “As if I could stop you.”

“I know, right?” A wide grin of triumph spread over her lips. “But it was sort of cute how you thought it was your decision.”

Lord, this woman. He really needed to wipe this stupid grin off his face.

She turned and headed down the hall. “I’ll get a quick shower while you grab that Glock,” she said over her shoulder, all cheerful smiles now that she’d gotten her way. “Meet you outside in ten.”

He stared after her, wondering how she always managed to tear down his guard with one sweet look in those huge, brown eyes. Of course he’d given her what she wanted; he didn’t stand a chance.

Now he was going to have to stick close and not let her out of his sight. Because despite everything, he’d promised God and his own heart that he would keep Ruby safe.

And he would keep that promise with his life.

SIX

"Score! I win!" Oliver broke into a victory dance, pumping his kid-sized plastic hockey stick in the air.

The little guy was allowed to play hallway hockey, provided he use a foam puck and plastic sticks. Normally, Ruby was the little guy's fiercest opponent, but until her injuries were fully healed, she played scorekeeper from her recliner in the living room.

"That's four goals for the Calgary Flames!" she said. "Good job!"

This was Oliver's third solo game in a row, and his youthful enthusiasm was buoying her spirits. It made Dex's imposed house arrest a bit less dreary and afforded Nate a respite from his nanny duties.

"I'm hungry, Ruby. Let's have lunch."

She adjusted her ice packs and stood. "Sounds good." She scraped her prepaid phone off the end table and slipped it into the pocket of her shorts. Luckily, Reyes and his deputies had recovered her go-bag from the bus station alley and brought it to the lodge, along with Dex's truck. "What would you like to eat?"

Oliver tilted his head to the side, thinking. "Peanut butter and jelly."

"Sounds good." She reached out her hand, and he wrapped

his sweaty little-boy fingers around hers, stealing yet another piece of her heart. Maybe it was selfish, but she thanked God she was here with him and Dex, not on some bus, alone, headed who knew where. Being at the ranch felt like home.

A dangerous delusion, she reminded herself grimly. Still, her rebellious heart beat a happy rhythm.

They walked hand-in-hand into the kitchen, Ruby scanning every window on the way. She was on a half-hour break—Dex insisted she take frequent rests for her body to heal, and Oliver demanded his playmate.

"What kind of jelly do you want, little man? Grape or strawberry?"

Oliver rushed past her to the refrigerator. "No, silly, *I'm* making lunch for *you*!"

She did a double take. "You are?"

"Yes!" He rummaged noisily until he found what he needed, then spun around with a huge little-boy grin on his face. "Uncle Dex told me to take care of you. He said you're not allowed to do any work while you're on break."

"That's right." Dex's smooth, deep voice had her turning toward the door, where he'd just walked in. He was ruggedly handsome in his jeans and button-down, the sleeves rolled up to reveal forearms tanned from the sun. In the yard beyond him, two patrol cars sat in the driveway.

Apparently, Dex and Reyes weren't taking any chances with her security.

Dex strode into the kitchen, his blue eyes locking on hers, a brooding look on his face. "Good man, Ollie." His gaze on Ruby never wavered. "I'll take it from here."

Oliver ran up to him and leapt into his arms. Dex tossed him over his shoulder, giggling and squirming, and deposited him on the couch. Oliver reached for the TV remote.

"Can I watch a show, Uncle Dex?" His wide eyes were hopeful.

Dex put his hands on his hips, his expression stern. "You have twenty minutes. Then you eat your sandwich and go back to playing."

Screen time was limited around Dexler Acres, where everyone was expected to spend their day working—or in Oliver's case, mostly playing.

"Thanks!" He flipped on the screen and was promptly transfixed.

Ruby's heart ached watching the two of them together, as close as father and son, and she wondered how Dex managed to be so good at the father-figure thing while also running a successful ranch.

He was sort of her superhero, but she scolded herself for the thought. He wasn't "her" anything.

"Let's see what we've got here." Dex surveyed the contents strewn over the kitchen counter. "Two PB&Js coming up."

Ruby lifted her chin. "I can make my own."

Dex made a tutting sound. "You need to rest, tough guy. Since you've insisted on playing guard duty—" his expression darkened with frustration "—you need to take breaks."

Ruby opened her mouth to protest but decided against it. The entire left side of her body was throbbing, so if her gorgeous boss insisted on pampering her, she wasn't going to argue.

"Thank you." She sat on a stool at the kitchen island and adjusted her multiple ice packs.

Dex shot her a stern look. "You should prop up that ankle."

She made a dramatic show of plopping her left foot up onto the stool next to her. "Do you realize how bossy you are?"

"Yes, I do." He tossed her a grin, the blue of his eyes dramatic against the deep tan of his skin. "Because you've told me many times."

"Just making sure you're aware."

His lips twitched up as he slathered bread slices with peanut butter and jelly. It felt good to banter like this, but tension still crackled between them, the secrets she'd hidden casting a shadow on their easy rapport.

He slid Ruby her plate. "How are you feeling?"

She took a bite of her sandwich, watching him from under her eyelashes. He was tall and imposing standing in front of her, physically strong from years of combat, rodeo riding, and ranching. He always seemed so confident and capable, but Ruby wondered if he had any hidden weaknesses, any chinks in his armor. She met his somber eyes, which were fixed intently on her.

"Sore, but better."

"You keeping your ankle wrapped?" he asked gruffly.

Her lips curved into a grin. "You know what? I've figured out something about you."

He quirked an eyebrow. "Oh, yeah? What's that?" He rounded the island separating them and stood before her.

"You're pushy because you care."

Surprise flickered in his eyes. He didn't respond right away, like she'd stunned him into silence. Still, he kept his gaze locked on hers and took a step closer. Heat poured off him, his body warm from the sun and hard work, radiating his fresh, spicy scent.

When he finally spoke, his voice came out rough. "Yeah, I do."

She swallowed hard, lost in the deep well of blue in his eyes.

He reached out and brushed a curl from her forehead, his

fingers rough and callused against her skin. A warm, pleasant shiver trailed up her spine.

"You see too much of me, Ruby. And it's getting harder to hide."

He let his fingers slide down the length of her hair, sending butterflies dancing through her stomach. He leaned closer, then suddenly tensed, like an invisible cable was pulling him back. He withdrew his hand sharply and looked away.

"I'm going with Sheriff Reyes to do a sweep of the property." His voice was clipped now, his expression detached. "We'll be back in about an hour."

Ruby's heart stuttered, thrown off beat by his sudden one-eighty. "O-kay. I hope all this security stuff isn't keeping you from getting your work done."

He'd been overseeing her around-the-clock protection, and she didn't want the ranch to suffer because of her.

"It's fine." He stepped away, avoiding her eye.

He was still angry that she'd lied to him. Not that his coldness should bother her. In a few days she would be out of his life anyway.

But it did. It hurt like crazy.

He turned for the door, but she grabbed his sleeve. He froze and slowly turned back, the hard set of his jaw contrasting with the hurt flashing in his eyes.

And it tore her heart to pieces. "Look, Dex, I… I didn't want to lie to you—"

"I know that," he broke in, his voice sharp. He let out a breath and dragged a hand down his face. "I know," he said, softer this time. "I just, uh, have some baggage from my past that isn't letting me—" the muscle ticked in his jaw "—isn't letting me get past this." He pressed his lips together. "Look, there was this woman a couple of years ago. I fell in love with her."

Ruby's jealousy flared, hot and painful, but she waited for him to continue.

"But she lied to me, too. She knew that, being an owner of a large ranch, I'm…successful. She wanted money from me. Small amounts at first, then bigger. Turns out, she was an addict using me to score her next high. She was beautiful and charming and hid her true nature well, but I eventually figured it out. I felt…" He looked away, his jaw muscle flexing. "Deeply betrayed. Even though I was no longer interested in being with her, I tried getting her help. But once she realized I wasn't funding her addiction anymore, she disappeared."

Ruby stared back at him, stunned to silence, her heart aching for him.

He swallowed hard. "I know you're not her, Ruby. I know you kept secrets from me for a good reason. I just can't… separate the two *here*." He pointed to his heart.

"Dex, I…" She stepped away, giving him space. "I understand."

"No, you don't." He stepped in closer, eradicating the gap she'd just created between them, his eyes flickering. "Because even though I can't trust you, I can't stay away from you. You draw me in. You're this…stunning light shining into all my dark places, and I would do anything…" He squeezed his eyes shut. "Ruby, I would do *anything* for you."

Ruby stared up at him, her heart racing, wanting to reach for him but afraid he would push her away.

He shoved his fist through his thick, glossy hair, looking lost. "I must have no sense of self-preservation."

She opened her mouth but quickly snapped it shut. What could she say? He was drawn to her yet unable to forgive her, and there was nothing she could do about that.

He stepped away, his cold mask slipping back into place. "Look, Deputies Lewis and Garcia are outside, but don't go wandering too far." He rapped his knuckles restlessly against the counter. "I gotta go."

"O-kay." The word came out as a choked whisper, but Dex had already turned his back and strode to the door. It slapped shut behind him, and a moment later, two ATVs roared to life.

A cold emptiness opened inside her, and her eyes filled with tears. For Dex, and what he'd gone through. For her own heart, denied what it had been secretly hoping for. She'd sacrificed so much these past ten years, seeking justice for her mother. Jude "Dex" Dexler was the latest notch in her tally of regrets.

And the most painful.

But of course she couldn't blame him, and it was for the best, anyway. Allowing herself to get attached while she was in WITSEC was naïve and selfish. She needed to remember her mission and stay focused.

Gathering the cracked pieces of her heart, she padded over to Oliver sprawled across the couch. She sat beside him and cuddled him close, seeking comfort in her fierce love for him. He nuzzled her back silently, engrossed in some cartoon flashing on the screen. Nate strolled in a few minutes later and joined them, plopping down beside the little guy. Ruby stood, feeling restless, and returned her ice packs to the freezer.

"I'll be right outside if you need me, Ollie Man." Even though the sheriff's deputies were keeping watch, she needed a distraction from all these swirling, tangled feelings in her heart.

She slipped on her boots and stepped outside. Out of habit, she brushed her fingers over the Glock holstered at her hip, the cool, hard metal reassuring.

Deputy Lewis stepped out of his cruiser and crossed the yard to join her. "How are you feeling today, Ms. Laurier?"

Like my heart's been torn to ribbons and trampled by a herd of cattle. But of course she couldn't say *that*.

She forced a smile. "Hanging in there."

Another cruiser was parked a couple hundred yards away, at the end of the driveway. Dex had told her Deputy Garcia would be watching the road while Deputy Lewis stuck closer to the lodge.

"I'm glad to hear it." Lewis grinned, revealing a dimple in his cheek. He had a round, boyish face, appearing even younger than his thirty years. He'd made conversation with Ruby when they were both outside patrolling earlier, showing her pictures on his phone of his wife and their new baby. "You've been through a lot. Even though Reyes won't tell us the details."

That was because Reyes didn't *know* the details, only that Ruby was in WITSEC and no longer trusted the US marshals. The sheriff didn't like the lack of information—and hadn't been shy about saying so—but had ultimately backed off his questioning because of his trust in Dex. Besides, Ruby was in his county and under his protection.

Lewis pulled his phone out of his pocket and looked at the screen. His youthful face went slack with surprise. "It's Reyes. He and Dex found something suspicious down by the riverbed."

Already? They'd only left fifteen minutes ago. Her heart crashed into her sore ribs, and she drew in a sharp breath. "What did they find?"

He studied his phone screen, which was too dark against the midday sun for her to read. "Footprints. He wants us to come check it out."

Ruby frowned. "Us? I'm not supposed to leave the house, and you're not supposed to leave Oliver and me alone."

The young officer shrugged. "Maybe that's why he wants me to bring you."

A pit opened in her stomach. "I won't leave Oliver."

Lewis smiled, but it seemed a bit...forced. "He'll be fine. Garcia's here, and there are half a dozen ranch hands milling around. He won't be alone."

A niggling suspicion carved a deeper and deeper pit in Ruby's stomach. She stepped closer to try to get a peek at Lewis's text message, but he slid his phone smoothly back into his pocket.

"C'mon." His tone was an octave higher than usual. "It won't take long. There are service roads all the way out to the river. We can take my cruiser."

He gestured to his vehicle parked a few feet away, and alarm bells clanged in Ruby's head.

Working undercover for the Bureau, she'd learned to trust her instincts. They'd kept her alive so far, and she wasn't about to ignore them now.

"No."

Lewis's boyish grin fell, and his features sharpened. "Ms. Laurier, Reyes has requested you come assist with this investigation. Are you going to refuse the county sheriff?"

She took a step back.

Lewis followed.

Her pulse kicked up, and she closed her hand over her Glock. "Show me Reyes's message." She'd thought the screen had looked dark because of the sunlight. But maybe it had looked dark because there was no message at all. The thought made the fine hairs on her neck stand on end.

The expression on Lewis's face turned frantic. "You don't believe me? Sheriff Reyes gave you a direct order! You can't refuse to cooperate!"

"Yes, I can." Her heart jackhammered. "I haven't done anything illegal, and I'm not one of his deputies."

Lewis was shaking. It was almost as if he were…afraid. But what was scaring him?

He gripped her arm. "My boss told me to bring you to him, and I will."

He pulled her toward his police car, but she yanked her arm back, sending a searing jolt of pain through her tender shoulder. "I'm not going anywhere with you!" She pulled her burner phone from her pocket to call Dex, and Lewis lunged for it.

"Give me that!" he yelled, dropping all pretense. "You're getting in my car, now!"

She veered out of his reach and swept his feet out from beneath him. He went down hard—but he wouldn't be down for long.

She punched out a quick text.

Lewis is forcing me into his car.

The phone flew out of her hands, followed by an explosion of pain. Lewis had kicked the phone out of her grip.

Ruby stumbled, reaching for her Glock, but Lewis was already on her. He fisted her hair and yanked her head back, then pushed the muzzle of his gun into her back.

"Walk." He shoved her toward his car.

She looked frantically at the other cruiser with Deputy Garcia inside. Had he noticed what was happening? Could she get his attention?

She opened her mouth to scream, but Lewis clamped his palm over her mouth and pressed his gun painfully into her kidneys. "One sound and I shoot."

Desperation flooded her. "Why are you doing this?" she demanded, her words muffled against his hand.

He kept shoving her forward. "I...have to. I'm sorry."

So, Walters was using him somehow. "Is someone paying you off?"

Maybe if she distracted him, she could buy time for Dex and Reyes to arrive. But what if Dex was busy, and he hadn't seen her message? *Lord, please let Dex be on his way.*

They reached the cop car and Lewis yanked open the door. "Get inside." His voice was strangled from the effort of shoving her.

Ruby could not allow him to push her into this car, gun in her back or not.

Because if she got locked into that cruiser, she was dead for sure.

A wordless prayer blowing through her mind, she went limp, making him temporarily lose his grip. She dropped low, ducked under his arm and started to run. Once she was a few steps away, she pulled her Glock from her waistband...

Arms clamped around her, as hard and strong as steel. Lewis pulled her back, shoved her into the side of the car and pressed his gun to her forehead.

"Do *not* even try," he growled between his teeth. "I will kill you now if you don't get into this car."

He was going to kill her anyway. Or take her to Walters's men, who would do the honors. She would already be dead if Deputy Garcia wasn't close enough to witness it.

Think, Ruby. Distract him. "Why are you doing this, Lewis?" Her voice shook. "You're a *sheriff.* You'll lose your job. You'll lose everything. Think about your family!"

His face went slack, his eyes burning with panic. "They'll *kill* my family if I don't cooperate!" His voice came out in a shriek of raw terror. "I have no choice!"

A creeping dread spread its icy tentacles through her belly. Walters would stop at nothing to silence her and save himself from the justice he deserved.

He was a ruthless monster, ready to harm an innocent woman and child to meet his ends.

“Please don’t do this,” she begged, her heart pounding and her limbs shaking. The cold, steel barrel of his gun reminded her that with one bullet, it would all be over. One squeeze of the trigger, and all hope for her mother’s justice would be blown to pieces.

She couldn’t scream for help. She couldn’t move. Lewis was no longer a trained, clear-thinking lawman. He was a terrified husband and father, willing to do anything to protect his family.

But Ruby still held her Glock in one hand. If she was going to die, it would be fighting, not cowering.

Lewis pushed the end of his gun harder into her skull. “Drop your weapon!”

Lord, deliver me.

Her gun low at her side, she pulled the trigger.

Lewis roared in pain and doubled over, gripping his thigh where the bullet had pierced him. Ruby spun away and took off at a sprint, heading for an ATV parked on the other side of the yard.

A shot cracked the air behind her, so close she squeezed her eyes shut and braced herself. What would a bullet feel like, tearing through her skin? Or would it sink into the back of her head and she’d feel nothing at all?

Even as her mind flashed through terrifying scenarios, her training took over. She zigzagged as she ran, making it harder for him to aim. She focused on survival as another part of her brain processed background information: A man was shouting. Not Lewis. The other sheriff. Garcia. He must have heard the gunshot and was running to her aid.

More engines revving. ATVs. She looked up to see Dex and Reyes burst out of the woods, barreling toward her.

Hope bloomed in her chest, but she didn't break stride as she altered course and raced to them. Help was on the way: Dex and Reyes in front of her, Garcia behind. But Lewis was still shooting, and a desperate man could not be underestimated.

Which would reach her first: Dex and the other officers or a bullet?

The scene before Dex's eyes made the blood freeze in his veins. When he'd received that alarming message from an unknown number, he'd instantly realized it was Ruby, texting from her burner phone. But why would Deputy Lewis force her into his cruiser? Dex had prayed there was a simple misunderstanding.

But there was no misunderstanding what he was looking at now: Ruby racing toward him, bullets following in her wake. Deputy Sheriff Lewis sprawled on the ground, injured, *shooting* at her.

Fear and rage and utter confusion slammed into him. Why was one of Reyes's trusted men trying to murder Ruby? What had made him turn?

Deputy Garcia pounded toward the other officer, gun drawn, shouting. He'd nearly reached Lewis, but Lewis was still firing, like he was desperate to kill Ruby at any cost.

"I'm going to help Garcia take down Lewis," Reyes shouted over the noise of the engines. "You cover Ruby."

Dex twisted the throttle and shot forward, determined to reach her. She was about fifty yards away now, close enough to see the pure panic etched on her face.

I'm coming, Ruby. Hang on.

He slowed at the last minute, grabbed her around the waist and hoisted her in front of him on the seat.

"Head down!"

For once, she didn't argue.

He hunched over, covering her with his body, then pulled the ATV around in a one-eighty, heading back to the cover of the woods.

Once they were shielded by the trees and thick foliage, Ruby lifted her head. "Stop."

Dex turned the ATV back around and cut the engine. They waited in silence for a minute, holding their breaths.

"No more gunshots," Ruby whispered.

A rush of emotion crashed into him. He pulled her into his arms and held her tight, murmuring her name over and over.

She turned to him and he swept his gaze over her face. "Tell me what happened."

"We need to check on Oliver first."

Dex was burning with questions but knew she was right. Even though his nephew was in the lodge, tucked away from immediate danger, he'd no doubt heard the commotion and was scared.

Dex twisted the throttle and headed for the ranch, his mind swirling with confusion. Lewis had been an exemplary deputy for the past three years, well before Ruby had shown up. That meant whoever was pursuing Ruby had manipulated him somehow. Money and fear were the usual methods, and Dex wondered which it was. Either way, Ruby's enemies were powerful—which he'd already surmised, since she'd been placed in WITSEC in the first place.

It seemed no one was beyond their reach.

They motored across the yard, where Reyes and Garcia

had overpowered Lewis. He was cuffed and sprawled on the ground, bleeding from one leg.

Over the rumble of the motor, Dex brought his lips close to Ruby's ear. "You shot him in the leg?"

Her muscles tensed against him. "I had to."

"I know." Dex curled an arm around her waist, silently reassuring her. He could tell violence unnerved her, because for all her feistiness and snark, she was a gentle soul. But he didn't want her second-guessing her actions or feeling the least bit guilty for protecting herself. Lewis hadn't given her the choice.

She leaned into his embrace, resting her back against his torso. Dex felt the tension melt out of her muscles, like his closeness calmed her. Suddenly, his heart felt too full. He wanted to be there for her, whenever she needed him. He wanted her to trust him with her safety, but also with so much more.

But could he trust *her*?

The thought was like a dark cloud slipping over the sun.

"Need a hand?" he called out to Reyes and Garcia.

Lewis didn't even look up or try to move. He was face down in the dirt, utterly defeated. Dex wondered if he felt guilt or regret. He didn't believe Lewis was an evil person—maybe just desperate and weak.

"Nah, reinforcements are on the way," Reyes called back. "Just take care of Ruby."

Dex tucked her even closer to him. "I intend to."

They pulled up to the lodge and Ruby climbed down, her limbs shaking. Dex offered her a hand, but of course she was too proud to take it. He followed as she rushed inside, only limping slightly, and made a beeline for Oliver.

The little man was still on the couch, curled into Nate's

side, eyes wide. "Is something wrong? I heard gunshots and yelling."

Dex exchanged a meaningful glance with Nate. "Give us a minute?"

"Sure, boss." He gave Oliver's shoulder a squeeze and stood. "You were brave, buddy."

He disappeared down the hall, and Ruby took his place beside Oliver. She gathered the little boy into her arms, too emotional to respond.

"Everything's okay now," Dex said, closing the distance between them. He sat on the other side of his nephew and gathered both him and Ruby in his arms. It felt good, the three of them together. Too good to be true.

"What's going on?" Oliver's voice was muffled against Ruby's shoulder.

Dex pulled in a deep breath. How much should he explain to his young nephew? He never wanted to lie to him, but there were some realities too harsh to unload on an eight-year-old. Dex had been thrust unexpectedly into the role of a father, and half the time he wondered if he was botching the job.

"A situation got out of hand," he said vaguely. "The sheriffs took care of it." There. An answer with no real information. Maybe he could run for political office.

"What happened?" Oliver pressed. "And why are the cops still here?"

Dex pushed a hand through his hair and caught Ruby's eye. She nodded, silently giving him permission to explain the situation. He let out a jagged breath and sank his gaze into hers. She was placing her trust in him, in spite of the danger she faced, and the honor of that trust was a balm on his soul.

"There's someone who wants to harm Ruby. So, we're looking after her."

Oliver's mouth dropped open. "Who wants to hurt Ruby?"

"I don't know," Dex said honestly. At least he had deniability there.

His youthful face scrunched up with worry. "Bad guys?"

"Yeah," Ruby whispered. "Bad guys."

Dex's heart ached. He cared deeply about these two people, and seeing them frightened ignited a white-hot protectiveness inside him. "We won't let anything happen to her though."

Oliver hugged Ruby closer. "Yeah, we won't let anyone hurt you, Ruby."

Dex's heart swelled with pride at his young nephew's love and courage. He reached out and mussed his hair, unable to find the words to express the intensity of his emotion.

Ruby squeezed her eyes shut and held Oliver tighter in her arms. "Thank you, Ollie Man." Her voice was choked with tears, but resolute. "I won't let anyone hurt you either."

Dex caught Ruby's glance and held it. "I'm sorry I left you with Lewis."

"Dex, this isn't your fault."

"I know that. Sort of." He scrubbed a hand down his face. "Either way, I'm going to make a promise to you now." He burned his gaze into hers. "I won't leave your side until this is all over."

She shook her head. "Dex, you have a ranch to run, and I've already pulled you away from your work too much—"

"I will *not* leave your side."

She grinned weakly. "What's your plan? Board up my bedroom window? Lock me in my room? Handcuff me?"

He wanted to grin back, but fear still had him in its stranglehold. He smoothed a hand down her hair, and she leaned into his touch. "Go where you like," he murmured, his eyes still locked on hers. "Do what you like. But I *will not leave your side* until you're safe."

Ruby drew in a sharp breath, those bottomless dark eyes

making his poor heart beat out of control. “The trial is only five days away.” She placed her hand over his, her fingers cool and soft against his skin. “This will be over soon.”

He was surprised to feel his heart sink. He wanted the *danger* to be over, not his time with her.

Ever.

She lied to you. She deceived you. You still *don’t even know who she is.*

Dex needed the reminder. He shook his head, clearing the sentimental cobwebs. His reckless heart was wandering away from all logic, setting him up for disappointment. Ruby would be gone in five days. He needed to accept that and keep her safe until then.

“You’ll make it to your trial.” He winced at the detached tone of his voice. “Reyes already offered a security detail to escort you to the airport. Until then, you’re stuck with me around the clock.” He stood and reached out a hand to help her up. “Why don’t you go lie down and rest for a bit?”

She took his hand and stood, but the expression on her face was anything but compliant. “You expect me to ‘go lie down’ after what just happened? My attackers are getting more brazen by the hour, and I’m not going to lock myself in my bedroom while you and Reyes risk your lives for me.”

Dex sighed. “Ruby, just *one time*, could you go easy on me?” Did he really expect his little fireball to do what he asked? It would have been a first in recorded history.

She lifted her chin. “I’m not trying to give you a hard time. I can help.”

He pushed a hand through his hair, frustrated. “Ruby, you’re a machine. You take down men twice your size. Trained men. Your abilities are not in question.” He took a step toward her and locked his gaze on hers, pleading. “But you, out there—” he gestured toward the yard “—is like waving a red flag at a bull. So, please…" He took her hand, her skin so soft against his. "Please make my job easier and stay inside."

She opened her mouth, no doubt to argue with him, when Oliver piped in.

"Will you please stay inside with me, Ruby?" His wide, innocent eyes implored her. "I don't want to be by myself. I feel scared."

She sucked in a sharp breath and gathered the little boy into her arms. "Ollie, you don't have to be scared." She cradled his head into the crook of her neck. "Of course I'll stay with you."

Dex dragged a hand down his face. "So, you'll listen to *him*, but not me."

To his surprise, she giggled. "I would do anything for my Ollie Man." She smoothed a hand over his glossy, messy hair, and he burrowed into her like a newborn puppy.

Dex's heart constricted seeing the two of them together. "It's because he's cuter, isn't it?"

"Yes!" Oliver answered, giggling.

Ruby's gaze slid to Dex's, a mysterious look in her deep, dark eyes. "Oh, I don't know about *that*, Jude Dexler."

His breath caught, and he wouldn't have been able to utter a word if he'd tried. That was not a casual look she was giving him. It was meaningful and heartfelt.

And his full name on her lips made his head spin like he was on the back of a bucking bronco.

It took him too long to respond. And based on the teasing grin on Ruby's mouth, she knew why.

He cleared his throat. "You enjoy torturing me, don't you?"

Her grin widened. "You make it too easy."

The sound of someone clearing their throat made Dex look up. Reyes stood in the doorway, a knowing grin on his face.

"Mind if I come in?"

Looked like Ruby wouldn't be resting just yet. "Of course. Have a seat." Dex gestured to the dining room table, then turned to Oliver. "Go play in your room for a while, Oliver. This is a grown-up discussion."

The little man's face fell with disappointment, but his uncle's expression left no room for argument. With one last, baleful look at the sheriff, he trotted off down the hall.

Dex threaded his fingers through Ruby's. "Ready for a few questions?"

She looked exhausted, her shoulders slumped, and her beautiful almond-shaped eyes were rimmed with shadows. His protective instincts raged, and he was tempted to tell Reyes to come back later. Of course, Ruby wouldn't have any of it; the rest, the coddling, or her boss's overly protective tendencies.

She squared her shoulders. "I'm ready."

So brave. He found himself grinning as she strode to the table, spine straight and eyes dry. She sat in a chair opposite the sheriff, and Dex lowered himself into the seat beside her.

Reyes's expression was sober as he settled his attention on Ruby. "I understand you gave Dex permission to tell me about your situation—or, at least the details he's aware of."

Dex caught the shaking of her fingers before she thrust them under the table. "That's right."

Reyes darted a glance to the driveway, where two more cruisers were pulling in. "One of my deputies attacked you, and the sheriff's department will investigate that. But rest assured that I will keep the, ah, *sensitive* details of your background private until you testify in a few days."

Ruby's posture went slack with relief, and when she spoke, her voice was barely more than a whisper. "Thank you, Sheriff."

Dex nodded at Reyes, a sign of silent understanding between them. Reyes was going to investigate this quietly, at least for now, to keep the pressure off Ruby. Dex thanked God for his friend, placed on their path at just the right time to help them.

Reyes straightened, pulling out a notepad. "So, Ms. Laurier, can you tell me what happened? From the beginning."

She shot a furtive look at Dex, and if he hadn't known better, he would have thought she was grateful he was there beside her. Maybe she needed him, just a little bit. The thought warmed him.

"Deputy Lewis told me you texted him, asking us to meet you out by the riverbed. He said you'd found some evidence you wanted me to look at. Alarm bells went off right away, since you and Dex had instructed me not to leave the lodge under any circumstances. Also, when he pulled out his phone to look at your alleged message, his screen was dark. There was no message at all."

Though he kept his professional demeanor, Reyes's eyes flashed with surprise. He noted everything silently in his notepad.

"When I refused to leave, he tried to push me into his car. He said someone threatened to kill his family if he didn't do it. I fought back and managed to slip away, and he fired shots at me. That's when Deputy Garcia realized what was happening and raced over to help. You and Dex showed up moments later."

Reyes exchanged a tense look with Dex. He leaned forward and lowered his voice to a murmur. "I understand, as a federally protected witness, you're not allowed to share information about your case, even to law enforcement. But from what Dex told me, you no longer trust the US Marshals

Service to protect you. That means the responsibility of your protection falls to Dex and me."

Dex reached under the table and grabbed her hand. It felt cold and clammy, so he brushed his warm fingers over hers, trying to settle her.

"In my position," Reyes continued, "some more details would be helpful, so we know what we're dealing with."

Ruby bit her lip, warring emotions in her eyes. She flicked a glance behind her, at the officers milling around the property, and lowered her voice. "The man who's pursuing me is desperate to prevent my testimony, because it will destroy his career and reputation. He's very powerful, with the reach and the resources to manipulate anyone, from US marshals to your own sheriff's department. So, I wish I could give you more information, and I wish I could reach out to WITSEC to whisk me away to safety, but there's not a single soul on earth that I trust." She swallowed hard. "Except Dex."

SEVEN

Ruby held her chin high and tried to maintain a brave face, but on the inside she was shaking like a leaf in the wind. She didn't distrust Reyes—he seemed like a good and honest man, and he'd gone out of his way to help her—but she couldn't disclose her or Walters's identity, period. The risk of a leak was too great. Walters was a public figure, the murder and fraud accusations against him all over the media. If word got out that the star witness testifying against him was hiding out in rural Montana, news outlets would start popping out of the bushes.

That would land her promptly in Walters's snares. The ruthless politician would pay generously for information, and that was too strong a temptation for many people.

But if she refused to talk, would Reyes withdraw his protection? Or worse, report her to US marshals who were potentially on Walters's payroll? A wave of ice-cold fear washed over her, and she stared back at the sheriff, awaiting his reaction.

But it was Dex who spoke. "Reyes, can you give us a minute?"

Reyes's gaze bounced between them, his expression unreadable. "Sure. I'll be outside."

The second he was out the door, Dex gripped the bottom

of her chair, swung it around to face him, and leaned in close, his eyes blazing into hers.

She held her breath. Was he angry she was still keeping secrets from them? Was he going to try to convince her to come clean to Reyes? She straightened her spine, preparing for a knock-down, drag-out confrontation.

Instead, he reached for her hands. "You trust me?" His voice was rough with emotion. "Only me?"

She blinked. That was not what she'd expected, and it took her a moment to respond. "Are you…mad?"

He released one of her hands to brush a curl from her cheek. The gesture was so gentle it made her heart roll over in her chest.

He leaned in closer, enveloping her in his warmth and fresh, spicy scent. "Why would I be mad?"

"Because I won't tell you and Reyes who's after me."

"Ruby." He recaptured her hand and brushed his thumbs slowly over her knuckles, his warm, rough skin rasping over hers and sending butterflies through her stomach. "You're doing your best to survive, and I get that. At least, I'm trying to get that. But if you're saying that you trust me, and the only reason you're not telling me your secret is because it's safer that way, then… I'll try and accept that." He pulled in a ragged breath, as if battling himself.

The kindness and sincerity of this man was too much. Ruby leaned in and pressed her forehead to his, needing to be close to him. To draw from his strength.

He drew in a sharp breath, reacting to her closeness. "Tell me again that you trust me," he murmured, the incredible blue of his eyes a blur sitting this close.

Emotion drowned her, and when she spoke, her voice was barely a whisper. "I trust you, Jude Dexler. Only you."

He squeezed his eyes shut and brought her hands to his chest, over his heart. "Then I'll trust you, Ruby Laurier."

She longed to tell him her real name, so he could say those words again, but to *her*. The real her. The impossibility of that made her heart ache.

He would never know the real her.

And yet, here he was, offering her unconditional trust and reassurance. What had she offered him in return? Lies, secrets, and trouble. The ache in her heart doubled, like it might crack right open.

"I don't deserve everything you're doing for me," she breathed.

He backed away just enough to look clearly into her eyes. "Well, I think you do. Besides, it doesn't matter what either of us think, because God decides what we deserve."

Ruby's lips tipped up, even as a fat tear slid down her cheek. Dex brushed it away gently with his finger, his intense gaze still locked on hers. "I'll protect you, Ruby."

She looked down. "Ruby's not even my name," she murmured, her voice snagging on a sob.

He tipped her chin up. "I know. But I'll protect you, anyway. And if one day you decide to tell me who you are, I'll be ready to listen."

The dam broke, and she lost it. She tipped forward, burying her face in his shoulder, and cried her heart out. For him, for Oliver, for the mother she'd lost, for *herself* that she'd lost, pretending to be someone else for so long. Someone who didn't even exist.

Dex didn't say a word, just rubbed gentle circles on her back and let her cry. She let the moment stretch on longer than she should have, but it felt so good for Dex to hold her. Too good for her own good. She'd be leaving in days, and her heart would pay the price for this embrace.

Finally, she pulled back and turned her face away, rubbing her eyes. Out of her peripheral vision, she noticed Dex frown.

"You all right, Killer?"

"Yeah, I just..." She scrubbed at her eyes, feeling self-conscious. "I look ugly when I cry."

He let out a hoot of laughter that sliced straight through her tension. "Do you know anyone who looks good when they cry?"

Despite her tear-streaked face and wet eyes, she turned to him and grinned. "No."

He took her hands again, and she laced her fingers through his. Warmth unfurled in her stomach like rays of sunshine, dispelling her self-doubt.

"If you're worried about how you look, let me reassure you." He lifted her hand and brushed his lips lightly over her palm. "You've got nothing to worry about."

Her stomach flipped at the contact of his lips, and she stared back at him, slack-jawed. He grinned, like he knew exactly his effect on her, and for a moment she forgot both her names.

Then she recalled there was a real problem she needed to worry about. "Do you think since I wouldn't give Reyes the information he wanted he'll refuse to help me anymore?"

Dex stiffened. "Reyes promised to protect you, just like I did. He wouldn't renege on his promise."

Ruby tensed, regret snaking up her spine. She hadn't meant to offend him or his friend. "But I wouldn't answer his questions. Plus, he's probably breaking every rule by helping me."

Dex's expression softened. "True and true. But he won't abandon you, Ruby. Reyes and I were both marines, and we're always faithful. I asked him to back me up, and he will. As for your other concern, he's not breaking any rules by protecting a citizen in his county. Someone has committed multiple attacks on this property, and he's working to apprehend the person responsible."

Ruby bit her lip. "You're sure?"

Dex brought her hand to his lips again. "You can count on him, Ruby. And you can count on me. You said you trusted me, right?"

Yes, she'd said that. It wasn't easy, though. Not after all these years living alone in the shadows and looking over her shoulder. Still, she nodded.

"So, trust me." He brushed a light kiss on her knuckle and stood. "I'll go handle Reyes."

Ruby wanted to go with him, but her heart was pulling her toward Oliver. With the danger swirling around them, she wanted him in sight. "Thank you."

She stood, adrenaline still trembling through her legs. Dex, who was still holding on to her hand, pulled her to him and sank his intense gaze into hers. "You can ugly cry on me whenever you need to."

Her lips tipped up. With Dex, she didn't have to always be strong and composed and in control. He'd seen her dirty, sweaty, bruised, sobbing—unconscious beside a dumpster!—and still here he was, looking at her like she was the most precious thing on earth. With him, she could be one hundred percent herself. Even if he didn't know her name, he knew *her.*

"Thank you." She pushed up onto her toes and wrapped her arms around his neck. His heart beat wildly against her.

He held her for a long moment before stepping back. "I'll go talk to Reyes."

"Okay." Her heart was racing, too, and her voice came out as thin as a reed.

His mouth tipped up in a boyish grin, and he strode out of the room, the back door slapping shut behind him.

It took Ruby a moment to recover her thoughts. "Oliver?" she called, heading down the hallway.

"In here!" he cried out from his bedroom.

She headed his way, stopping in her room to grab some hair clips from her dresser. With trembling fingers, she pinned her hot, sweat-dampened curls away from her face. *Better.*

She walked into Oliver's room to find him and Nate fiddling with an electric train set.

"You have lunch yet, Nate?"

The young man grinned good-naturedly. "Nah, but I'm fine. I'll grab something in a little while."

"You've got to be hungry. Go eat. Besides, I want to hang out with Ollie for a while."

Oliver beamed up at her.

Nate stood. "Maybe I'll eat with the other guys at the bunkhouse, if you don't mind?"

"Not at all." Nate was so mature and responsible, it was easy to forget he was a teenager, and he probably missed hanging out with the other ranch hands.

He reached down and mussed up Oliver's hair. "You sure?"

"Of course. Take your time." She shooed him off and sat down beside her little man on the floor. His room was bright and airy, decorated in a sports theme, with sunshine and fresh air pouring in through an open window. At least the space felt cheerful, since he would be relegated to indoor play for a while. With armed attackers circling, running around outside was no longer an option.

Ruby's heart pinched painfully. Logically, she knew it wasn't her fault that people were trying to kill her. But Oliver was tangled up in her problem, and that made her feel guilty.

And terrified.

He set down the train engine he'd been tinkering with and looked up at her. "Want to play soccer in the yard?"

His youthful face was so hopeful, it killed her to disappoint him. She pressed her lips together and shook her head. "Sorry, Ollie Man. Until this mess is sorted out, we need to stay inside."

His wide, brown eyes pleaded with her. "But there are cops everywhere! We'll be fine."

Regret stabbed at her heart. "Sorry, buddy. It's just not safe." She reached for the engine he'd placed on the floor. "Would you show me your train instead? It looks really cool."

He hesitated, but ultimately the prospect of showing off his toy won him over. "It's electric. Uncle Dex and I built it together. See, if you push this button here..."

He launched into a lengthy explanation, carried away by his typical enthusiasm, the soccer game forgotten. Ruby listened with a smile, grateful for the eight-year-old's distractibility.

The sound of the back door opening and the thud of Dex's boots made her turn, and her face flushed. She knew the sound of his steps. The way he moved.

The low rumble of his voice and the feel of his lips on her skin.

"Ruby!" he called from the living room.

She sucked in a sharp breath, flustered by her wandering thoughts. "Uh...be right back, Ollie."

The little guy spared her a glance before returning his attention to his train.

She walked down the hall, her heart thudding against her rib cage. What had Dex discussed with Reyes? Was the sheriff going to demand answers in return for his protection, despite Dex's reassurance? If he backed her into a corner like that, what would she do? What would Dex do?

Would Dex kiss her again, but on the lips this time?

Not important, she scolded herself. *Get your head in the game.*

Dex stood in the entryway, his height and the width of his shoulders filling the doorframe behind him. His eyes flashed when he caught sight of her emerging from the hallway, the intensity of his gaze contradicting the stoic set of his jaw. Was he remembering their moment together, too? Did he regret it? Since he'd discovered the secrets she was hiding from him, he'd become impossible to read. Hot then cold, attentive then withdrawn. His mercurial moods made her head spin, though she couldn't really blame him.

"Want to sit down?" The gravelly timbre of his voice sent electricity down her spine.

She headed toward the couch and lowered herself onto a cushion. "Is it bad?" She looked up at him with dread.

He furrowed his brow. "Of course not. Why would you think that?" He sat on the cushion on the other end of the couch.

As far away from her as possible. Her heart sank. Yeah, he definitely regretted his moment of weakness with her. Was it because he was still angry or because he had no feelings for her?

She brushed the dismal thought aside because there were more important problems to tackle. Her feelings had been secondary to her survival for the past decade, and that wasn't about to change now.

She shrugged. "You seem unhappy after talking to Reyes. I thought maybe something was wrong."

"No, ah..." He roughed a hand over his face. "Nothing's wrong."

That didn't sound reassuring. Ruby held her breath, her mind racing with doubt.

He moved to the cushion beside her, his Adam's apple bobbing. "Sorry if I alarmed you. I was just…brooding, I guess."

She tilted her head to the side. They faced multiple sources of worry, so he was going to have to be more specific. "Brooding about what?"

Silence stretched on for so long she thought he wouldn't answer.

"You," he finally said. He lifted those clear blue eyes to hers, and her heart stuttered. "It's frustrating not knowing who you really are."

Ruby's breath snagged in her throat. He was so sincere, and all she gave him in return was more questions. She caught her lower lip between her teeth, unsure what to say. "Look, Dex, I can't—"

"I know." He took her hand in his and traced lazy circles over her palm. "You don't need to say anything. This isn't about me pumping you for information." He threaded his fingers through hers, and his eyes darkened. "I'm just protective of the people I care about. You're in that category."

Warmth rushed through her. All those times he'd been gruff and overprotective, watching over her even though it raised her hackles…

It was because he cared.

She let out a shaky breath. "I care about you, too." She skimmed a finger over his hand, rough from hard work and padded with muscle. "I'm trying to protect you and Oliver, too."

"I know," he said. He leaned closer, like he could shield her from everything.

She pressed her lips together. "Even though I'm failing miserably."

"You're not. You're…" He swallowed hard. "A light in our lives. And the way you love that little boy…" The look he swept over her face made a swarm of butterflies flutter through her stomach. "I know it's real."

His words filled her soul to the brim, and she squeezed his hand tight. She opened her mouth to reply when a dampened thud and the sound of a scuffle carried down the hallway.

From Oliver's room.

They both froze, their bodies tense.

"Ruby?" a melodic, mocking voice sang out. "Ruby, come here. Someone wants to see you *very* badly."

Ice-cold adrenaline streaked through Dex's veins as he shot to his feet. He raced down the hall, aware of Ruby pumping forward at his side, just as desperate as he was to reach the little boy. Even as Dex's body reacted, his mind attempted to process what was happening. How had someone broken into Oliver's room without anyone seeing?

He burst into his nephew's bedroom, Ruby at his heels, and pure terror flooded him.

A huge guy in a sheriff's uniform—not quite the Cooper County standard issue, but close enough to fool anyone from a distance—held his eight-year-old nephew with a gun to his head.

It was the mountain of a man from the SUV attack two days ago.

Oliver squirmed in the attacker's grip, a gag over his mouth, and behind them, the bedroom window gaped open... just enough for a large man to squeeze through.

So, the attacker had disguised himself as a sheriff's deputy and climbed in through the window. With the handful of unfamiliar deputies from a neighboring county here to assist, it wouldn't have been hard to blend in.

Dex's muscles tensed with panic and frustration. He should have foreseen this possibility. He should have kept Oliver in sight, at all times. But he'd thought the significant police presence surrounding the lodge would keep them safe. He'd thought—

But there was no time for regrets and second-guessing. He lunged, but the huge man leaped back, dragging Oliver with him. The safety on his gun clicked, and Dex froze.

"Come any closer and I'll shoot!" the man barked. "Weapons on the floor! Both of you!"

Despair welled in Dex's heart. They had no choice; they had to give up their weapons.

But he wasn't about to hand over his nephew to this cold-blooded killer. He would find a way to protect him *and* Ruby. He had to.

Lord, show me a way.

Slowly, Ruby lowered her weapon to the floor. Then, to Dex's horror, she put up her hands and stepped toward the gunman. "I'll come with you." Her voice was shockingly steady. "Hand over the boy."

"Ruby!" Dex cried, trepidation burning through his veins like wildfire. "Don't—"

"It's the only way," she said softly, keeping her eyes locked on her attacker.

"Your gun, too!" the man yelled at Dex, his voice high with fear. "Throw it on the floor, now!"

He kept an arm locked around Oliver, whose full, little-boy cheeks were wet with silent tears.

Rage boiling inside him, Dex slid his weapon from its holster slowly; any sudden movement could spook this guy and push him to do something rash.

Like shoot Oliver and Ruby.

Dread blew through Dex's body like an icy wind. If this monster killed the two people who meant the most to him, he'd never recover. And he'd never forgive himself.

He let his Glock clang to the floor.

“Now let the little boy go,” Ruby said, her voice sharp as a blade.

The man’s eyes narrowed. “Not quite yet. On your knees.”

Dex’s pulse roared in his ears, and the primal need to attack this man nearly overwhelmed him. But the scum currently held his nephew at gunpoint, so he swallowed his instincts and bided his time.

Ruby dropped to her knees, her expression neutral.

Always the professional.

Still holding Oliver, the man pulled a set of zip ties from his pocket and handed them to Ruby.

“Tie up your wrists,” he ordered her.

Dex watched Ruby silently obey, thinking this guy could have just shot her on the spot, but that the sound of a gunshot would have brought a swarm of cops. He wouldn’t have made it ten feet before being tackled and cuffed.

So, he planned to take Ruby quietly, then dispose of her far away from a police presence.

But not if Dex had anything to do with it.

Her hands bound in front of her, Ruby nailed the man with a frosty, lethal glare. “Now, let the boy go.”

The man hesitated, clearly afraid to part with his bargaining chip, but the promise of retribution in Ruby’s eyes ultimately frightened him more.

With a rough shove, he sent Oliver stumbling toward Dex. Dex caught him under his arm and pulled him close. Half of his heart melted with relief, the other half burned with fury as he contemplated Ruby on her knees, wrists bound, head pitched forward…

Her next move took Dex’s breath away.

With her bound hands, she gripped the giant man’s ankle

and yanked, sweeping his feet out from under him. Taken off guard, he dropped like a load of bricks on the floor.

She'd bought them a window of time, and Dex wouldn't waste a second of it.

He sprang forward and brought his heavy work boot crashing down onto the man's wrist. With a grunt of pain, he dropped his gun and Dex kicked it away.

He pulled Oliver aside, gripping him by his thin shoulders. "Go get Sheriff Reyes!"

Oliver nodded, still gagged, and took off running.

Dex stepped in front of Ruby, blocking her from the attacker. "Go with Oliver!" he cried, desperate to get her out of harm's way so he could eliminate the threat.

She hesitated, her need to protect him *and* Oliver warring in her eyes.

"Ruby, please go!" Dex pleaded. Their attacker was almost on his feet again, and Dex couldn't have her anywhere near him. He bent to retrieve the gun he'd dropped.

She turned to go just as the man launched himself at Dex with the strength and bulk of a grizzly bear.

And two more armed men poured through the open window.

Dex recognized them as the other two attackers from the SUV. They were dressed in fake sheriff uniforms, too, and their intent was clear as they headed straight for Ruby.

"No!" Dex fired his Glock, striking the big guy in the hip. He cried out in pain and dropped, but the other two assailants rushed Ruby, one locking his hands around her waist, the other gripping her arms.

They yanked her toward the open window like a rag doll.

Ruby was scrappy and strong, squirming and kicking like a bronco, but fighting two big dudes on her own—with her hands tied—her chances were slim. And Dex couldn't take a shot at either man without risking hitting her.

Dex holstered his Glock and slammed into the man gripping Ruby's waist. The guy staggered but held on, and Dex rained punches down on his face, desperate to free Ruby from his grasp. When the guy couldn't take any more, he released Ruby to throw a punch.

Big mistake.

Ruby swung around and landed a powerful kick at her other attacker's chest, sending him careening back.

Dex shoved the other guy off, unsheathed his Glock and took aim.

Bang! The guy staggered backward and slid down the wall, gripping his arm. Dex blinked twice, confused. He hadn't pulled the trigger…

Reyes stood in the doorway, gun trained on their attackers.

A handful of deputies flooded the room…

Just as the third attacker pulled Ruby out the window, screaming and twisting wildly.

She managed to kick the gun out of his hand, but with her wrists bound, he overpowered her easily.

"Ruby!" Dex lunged for the window, reaching it before any of the deputies. He leapt out, gun drawn, just as the man tossed Ruby onto the back of an ATV and sped off toward the woods.

EIGHT

Ruby flailed and struggled against her captor's grip, trying to throw herself off the ATV, but his arm clamped around her like an iron band, pinning her bound hands to her torso.

She'd managed to kick away his gun, but his strength was still triple her own. He sat behind her, driving with one hand while he held her easily immobilized with the other. She tried to not let her spirits deflate with despair.

She was smaller, unarmed, and alone, but the Lord was on her side.

Plus, she had Dex. She kept her ears peeled for the rumble of another ATV—Dex had several others he used for the narrow trails snaking through his extensive property. The cops had been using them to monitor the open prairie, though they were currently parked in the barn.

But with every minute that ticked by, fear and confusion weakened her hopes. Dex and the police should have been right behind them, giving chase. Where were they?

Then a chilling thought struck her. Had her attackers slashed the tires on the other vehicles? Their police uniform disguises were well planned; maybe they'd thought to increase their chances of escape by incapacitating Dex's other ATVs. The deputies still had their cruisers, but vehicles that size couldn't fit through the narrow, wooded trails.

Ruby's throat closed so tight she could barely pull in a breath. Was she truly alone, out here with her abductor?

His phone vibrated against her. Maintaining his tight grip around her arms, he pulled out his cell with his other hand, then spoke with the phone tucked into the crook of his shoulder.

"I have her." Pause. "No, I lost my gun, and the cops showed up." Another pause, and his body went rigid against her. Ruby had a feeling whoever was on the other line was *not* happy about that development. "Okay," he said shakily after a moment. "I'll meet you there."

So, he was taking her to Walters, or at least to his hired guns. There were several access points to roads around the perimeter of Dex's property. No doubt his armed associates would be waiting at one of them.

And they would make sure she wouldn't live to testify in five more days.

She needed to figure out a way to escape. Thanks to Dex and Sheriff Reyes, who had eliminated the other two men, she would be fighting one on one. Even if she was facing a bigger, stronger adversary, these were the best odds she would get if they were going to meet up with more of Walters's men.

Trees whipped past her as they headed deeper into the woods. The air felt cool and dense with humidity as shade darkened the trail, and the smell of rain tingled in her sinuses. She glanced up at the tiny pockets of sky she could spot through the gaps in the trees. Fat, dark clouds hung low, heavy with rain, and electricity filled the air.

A storm was gathering.

She tightened her fists, wondering if she could pull her hands loose from his grip…

"Don't try anything stupid," he snarled, his voice low and

threatening. "It'll be easier for you if you sit nicely, like a good girl."

Oh, *heck* no. She would not be making his job any easier. She would fight him tooth and nail.

Especially tooth…

She dropped her chin and sank her teeth—hard—into the arm he kept pinned around her.

He bellowed in pain and rage, his grip loosening slightly.

But before she could exploit the advantage, she was shoved roughly forward and her head crashed into the steering column. Pain exploded in her forehead and shot all the way through to the back of her skull. The trees danced and swirled before her eyes, and darkness crept into the edges of her vision. Heavy oblivion threatened to blot out her thoughts, but she clung desperately to her consciousness. If she wanted to survive this, she needed to keep her head clear.

Her abductor tightened his hold, her arms still clamped against her stomach, and pressed his legs tightly around hers like a vise. The only weapon left at her disposal was her head, which floated dizzily over her shoulders.

Lord, give me strength.

With a deep breath, she dragged her head forward, gathering momentum, and sent it crashing back into her assailant.

With their height difference, the blow struck his chin. Not ideal, but it was enough to snap his head back with a crack of fissured bone. His steel grip across her body eased, and she wriggled her arms free, twisted at the waist, and sent her bound hands crashing into his face like a baseball bat.

He dodged at the last second and her knuckles only glanced his temple.

And made him angry.

He grunted like a hostile animal and grasped at her, fumbling to keep hold of the wheel and capture her attached wrists with one hand.

But Ruby was quicker.

Flexing the muscles in her core, she drew her knees up, pivoted to face him, and thrust her feet forward in an explosive kick to her captor's face. His head flew back violently and he let out a muffled grunt. Blood streamed from his nose and lip, and for the space of a second, his eyes lost focus.

He recovered quickly though. His hand shot out, quick as a snake, and closed around her wrists in an iron grip. Rage and evil burned in his eyes, a silent promise that her defiance would be punished.

A streak of lighting cleaved the sky; a brilliant flash of silver threading through the heavy gray clouds.

Boom! Ear-splitting thunder followed right after, vibrating through her chest like a drum. The storm was close.

The man squeezed her wrists painfully. "Stop fighting me!" he roared over the thunder and gusting winds.

Using the strength in her back and shoulders, she sent an elbow crashing into his nose. Bone cracked again and blood gushed from the wound like a hot, red geyser.

Fury contorted his features, and Ruby knew he was losing control. She needed to act fast, before he sent all that unfettered rage slamming down on her. She might not survive it.

She reached for the wheel, yanked it to the side, and the ATV spun wildly. Out of instinct, the man released her to grip the wheel, and she leapt from the vehicle.

Ruby tucked her body into a ball just before she struck the hard, dirt path. A bolt of searing pain shot up her injured ankle, and with a knot of panic she realized she'd reinjured her partially healed sprain.

Her head struck a raised root, and stars exploded behind her eyes as momentum rolled her away from the ATV.

Her head was pounding, her bruised shoulder and ribs were screaming, and the piercing pain in her ankle made her fear she wouldn't be able to walk, let alone run, away from her attacker.

But she was out of his grasp. She glanced up to see the ATV several feet ahead, toppled on its side. Her attacker lay beneath it, his leg pinned to the ground. New hope washed over her. Her odds of escape had just lifted dramatically.

But he was strong, and he wouldn't stay trapped under the ATV for long. She needed to move.

Gritting her teeth against the pain throbbing through her body, she slowly stood, balancing all her weight on her uninjured foot. She wobbled, unable to throw out her bound hands for balance. She tossed a look over her shoulder. Her gaze clashed with her attacker's, and his eyes narrowed with rage.

"You're going to regret that! I'm coming for you!"

Fear pierced her like a knife. If he got his hands on her again, he was going to hurt her. Badly.

Or worse.

She needed to put distance between them, no matter how painfully her body protested. Bracing herself, she took a step toward the trees.

She'd known it would hurt, but she wasn't prepared for the explosion of white-hot agony that ripped through her joint. She bit her lip to keep from crying out, hiding her weakness from the predator that was hunting her.

She hobbled toward the cover of trees, the pain so excruciating she nearly passed out. Her head dizzy and her ruined joint threatening to give out, she pushed herself into the woods, farther from her pursuer and deeper into the thick forest.

Her cell phone bulged in her shorts' pocket—the burner phone Reyes had recovered from her go-bag—and she clumsily reached for it with both hands. Her pursuer was right behind her and she didn't have much time, but she needed to send Dex her location. She scrambled to click on her navigation app, praying she would have a signal out here in the middle of nowhere.

The app opened, and her heart fluttered with relief. She quickly dropped a pin on her location, sent it to Dex, and kept moving forward.

Every step was a burning, dizzying torture. Despite her iron will, her pace was slowing. Any moment, her body would cease to obey her brain and she would collapse on the forest floor, a sitting duck.

A dampened clang of metal resounded from behind her. The man had managed to push the ATV off his leg. Had the crash injured him? Would it slow him down? Ruby had a feeling he wasn't going to let pain deter him either. If he returned to Walters without her, he would be in a whole *world* of hurt.

He was as desperate to reach her as she was to escape him.

She took another step and her ankle buckled beneath her. Unable to throw her arms out, she struggled to regain her balance before the hard, rocky ground rushed up to meet her. Swallowing past a sob, she leaned against a tree, her mind grasping wildly for a solution.

Lord, how am I going to get out of this mess? Please show me a way.

She scanned her surroundings, and her eyes landed on a couple of thick branches, each about four feet long.

That's it. Her spirits buoyed. *Crutches.*

Trouble was, she needed two free hands to grip them. Her buoyed spirits took a nosedive…until a thought flickered in her mind.

Her hairpins.

Were there any left in her hair after her wild ride through

the woods? She sank her fingers into her thick, disheveled locks, feeling around blindly until her fingertips brushed against the head of a bobby pin. Would it be the right size to unlock the ties? Only one way to find out.

She pulled out the pin, inserted it into the head of the zip tie around her wrists, and pushed down on the locking mechanism.

It released.

Tears of relief sprang to her eyes. She pulled the ends loose and tucked the ties into her pocket. Then her gaze found the branches again.

They lay beside a fallen tree just ahead, but her abused ankle wouldn't bear one more step.

Leaves crunched about a hundred yards behind her. Footsteps. The man was getting closer.

She ducked behind the tree and quieted her breaths. There was no way he could see her in the dense woods, but he would hear. She would need to move in absolute silence.

Slowly, she sank to the ground on one foot. She was grateful for her years of physical training, as well as her daily work on the ranch that made her strong and nimble. Avoiding leaves or branches or anything that would crunch under her weight, she crawled noiselessly to the branches.

The ground was softer and damper here than on the packed trail, the loose earth filled with sharp rocks and twigs. By the time she reached the branches, her hands and knees were scraped and bleeding and caked with dirt.

But adrenaline propelled her forward, and she wrapped her palms around the thick, sturdy wood and sank the tips into the soft ground.

"Ruby!" the man taunted from behind her, his voice so close her heart seized with panic. "I know you're here somewhere!"

Her pulse thundering in her ears, she gripped the branches, braced her weight against them, and pushed herself up.

"Ruby Laurier!" he called out, his voice mocking. "Or should I say Isadora de la Cruz? Come out here and see me."

Another streak of lightning lit up the sky and thunder boomed right behind it. A fat drop of rain plopped down on her forehead, followed by another.

Then the skies opened and a deluge battered down on them.

Water flooded her vision, but it was a blessing from Heaven. Her pursuer wouldn't be able to hear her footsteps in the pelting rain.

Lord, command nature's elements to conceal me, she prayed. *Rain them down on my enemy.*

Bracing herself on her makeshift crutches, she picked her way around trees, rocks, and roots. Her drenched clothes stuck to her skin, sweat mixed with rain stung her eyes, and her scraped, muddied palms slipped clumsily over her crutches.

But she made progress.

She prayed the police were out there somewhere, searching for her, but no sounds of engines or voices penetrated the clamor of the rain.

They *were* out looking for her, right? If not on ATVs, then on horseback, or at least on foot…

She had no idea.

She also had no way of knowing how close her pursuer was, since she couldn't hear anything over the roar of the storm. Maybe it was intuition, maybe it was paranoia, but she could *feel* him close by. Narrowing the precious gap between them.

She had no choice but to keep moving and trust in the Lord.

The deeper she penetrated the woods, the darker her path grew. Heavy tree cover and black thunderclouds blotted out the light, and she hobbled blindly along the rocky, root-pocked ground. The rain pounded down harder, muddying the path and pouring into her eyes. Her hands busy with her crutches, she didn't dare stop to wipe away the raindrops, choosing speed over caution. Praying she wasn't walking in circles.

Deprived of vision, her imagination conjured nightmarish images of the man leaping out from behind and grabbing her. Jumping from a bush and pushing her to the wet ground. Her heart raced and her throat closed up tight with panic, terrified she would bump into him at any moment.

She quickened her pace, brow furrowed against the pain, her path a blur in front of her. Suddenly, one crutch clipped a rock and lost purchase. Her hands slipped on the wet, slimy, wooden branches and her feet fell out from beneath her. Her full weight slammed down on her injured ankle, shredding the joint and sending a wave of dizzying agony through her body.

Then she was falling, her arms pinwheeling uselessly.

She crashed onto the muddy ground, her knee striking a jagged rock. One crutch skittered away then rolled down a hill. The other splintered down the middle.

Splayed out on her belly, she nearly screamed in frustration, but a sob choked her instead. All of this was futile, an exasperating, excruciating waste of energy and hope. Walters had murdered her mother. He'd hurt so many others. And now he was going to kill her, too. He'd taken everything she loved, torn her identity from her, and nothing—nothing—would stop him.

"Isadora!" the man called out in a singsong voice, taunting her. "I know you're close. Come out and see me."

Her iron will, that driving force inside her to survive, collapsed. Why keep battling this unstoppable force, like shaking a stick at a hurricane? It was useless and exhausting, so why not just lie down in the mud and accept what fate had apparently decided?

Then she thought of Dex's face, desolate as he'd watched her dragged outside by her attacker. She thought of Oliver's wide, innocent eyes filled with horror when that mountain of a brute had grabbed him and pointed a gun to his head.

She cared deeply about both of them. And she was pretty sure they cared about her, too. Maybe she could give up on herself, but she wouldn't give up on *them*. A ray of strength poured through her, and her hopelessness evaporated like a puddle in the sun. Yes, she was beaten and broken and scared, but her God was with her, making her strong. All her years of training had prepared her for this challenge, and she wasn't going to lie down in the mud and die.

She was going to fight, and she wasn't alone.

Lord, be by my side.

Her crutches were destroyed, along with her ankle. She wouldn't be outrunning anyone in her current state. Her best option was to hide.

Dragging herself up to her knees, her body screaming in protest, she crawled to a dense thicket of vegetation. She pulled her phone from her pocket, hovered over the screen to protect it from the sheets of falling rain, dropped another pin on her location, and shared it with Dex.

She squeezed her eyes shut. *Dex, please see my messages. Please come for me.*

He knew this property better than anyone, every square foot internalized in his mind. But if he was stuck at the ranch with no operable ATVs, how could he reach her before her assailant, who was possibly only steps away?

Would Dex be able to find her at all, hidden in a dense forest blurred by sheets of rain?

She slid the phone back into her soggy shorts, dragged her

knees up to her chin, and waited, her pulse pounding with trepidation. Her survival came down to one question.

Who would find her first, Dex or her attacker?

Dex's heart hammered wildly, rage and desperation streaking through his veins. He pressed his heels into Skinny's flanks, urging the colt forward through the blinding rain.

"Yah!" he cried, even as the skittish horse hesitated under the relentless downpour. "Faster, boy!"

When he and Reyes had discovered that his ATV tires had been slashed, he'd raced to the horse barn. None of the police cruisers would fit through the narrow trails threading his property, and a search by foot wouldn't get him to Ruby in time. He'd burst into the barn to find Ruby's loyal colt, Skinny, his huge eyes rolling frantically and his hooves impatiently stomping the ground, as if he'd known his favorite human was in trouble.

Dex hadn't bothered with a saddle. He'd led the horse outside, leapt onto his back, and taken off like a shot across the prairie.

Now he was flying full-tilt toward the GPS pin Ruby had sent him. He didn't know how she'd managed to send him a message. Had she somehow escaped? But the fact that she hadn't called probably meant she was afraid her captor would hear her. She could be on the run, or holed up somewhere, hiding.

God, please don't let these monsters take her away from me. Please keep her safe until I reach her.

Razor-sharp protectiveness slashed through his body as he guided Skinny around a hairpin turn. Trails zigzagged through his woods like a system of arteries, and Dex knew every angle and connector. He would find Ruby. He would keep her safe, just like he'd promised.

Unless he didn't get to her in time. Unless the man was hurting her right now.

Dex's limbs trembled with panic, but he shoved aside the creeping worry, forcing himself to focus. Tightening his grip on Skinny's reins, he clamped his legs around his flanks and urged him forward. The colt responded immediately, like he was just as eager to race to Ruby's aid.

Ruby's abductor had a head start, but the trails were tight and twisting and would be difficult for the guy to follow, whereas Dex knew them like an extension of his body. No doubt Ruby's kidnapper would need to slow his pace to maneuver the ATV through the sinuous trails, which meant Dex could close the gap. And with the roar of the ATV's engine, he might not hear the pounding of Skinny's hooves until Dex was right behind them. The thought sent a glimmer of hope through the darkness of his thoughts.

Dex's Winchester was slung across his back and his Glock was tucked into his hip holster. He would gallop up from behind, get them in range and make that coward wish he'd never even glanced Ruby's way.

Dex leaned forward, using his body cues to push Skinny faster. He wanted to cry out Ruby's name, but that would alert her abductor to his presence.

A loud crack of thunder shook the air. Skinny reared up on his hind legs and squealed in distress.

"Easy, Skinny." Dex forced calm into his voice despite the urgency streaming through his veins. "Keep moving, boy."

Skinny hesitated only a moment before obeying Dex's commands. Compared to bareback bronc riding at rodeos and taming unbroken range horses, Skinny's gentle reluctance gave way like butter to a hot knife.

"That's it, Skinny," he praised, pressing his heels into the horse's flanks. "Faster, boy."

The horse shot forward, hooves battering the rocky path, drawing closer to Ruby's location. Dex's muscles tensed in anticipation. His fists tightened around the reins, his body humming with impatience to crush this person threatening Ruby.

More thunder rumbled and Skinny tried to slow, but Dex urged him on at an unrelenting pace. He slipped the Glock from its holster as he rode, the metal smooth and hard in his hand.

He blinked away the raindrops pelting his eyes and squinted past the gray blur of the trail in front of him.

A dark lump of metal materialized ahead. The ATV was flipped on its side on the edge of the trail, deserted.

No one in sight.

Panic flowed through his veins like an icy current. He leaped off Skinny, rushed to the scene of the crash, and scanned the ground. Traces in the mud showed where they'd fallen: a large imprint where the man had landed beside the vehicle, and a smaller trail leading a few feet away, indicating Ruby had either slid or rolled from the vehicle. Had she been thrown off or had she jumped? Dex's heart leapt into his throat, choking him. She'd already been injured by these monsters. Flying off a moving ATV would have crushed her still-healing wounds.

His fist tightened around his Glock, and his body quaked with rage. The moment he got his hands on this guy…

Focus, Dex. Unfettered anger would only muddle his thoughts, and he needed to think clearly to help Ruby. He dropped to a squat and studied the ground near Ruby's landing. Small footprints led into the woods, followed by larger ones.

She'd managed to escape her abductor, but he was hunting her. Dread gripped Dex in a stranglehold. Had the man already reached her? She was smart and quick, but her injuries must be slowing her. It would only be a matter of time before her pursuer bridged the gap.

Dex needed to move fast.

Gripping his wet, slick weapon in his hand, he scanned the woods. Sheets of rain reduced visibility to mere feet and dampened any sound. But Dex had tracked enemies through every terrain and condition as a Raider. He'd faced dangerous, high-priority missions vital to the safety of his country, but even then, the stakes hadn't been this high: he needed to rescue the one woman he couldn't live without.

He slipped between the trees, following the trace of footprints in the wet earth which seemed to lead in the direction of the GPS pin. The footsteps were close together, the right sunken deeper than the other. So, she was limping. Dex's rage boiled over. This man had hurt her, and he intended to do even worse. His larger, deeper footprints pursued hers, spread far apart, like he was walking fast or even running. Dex deduced that he was uninjured from the crash.

Well, that was about to change, the moment Dex got his hands on him.

Dex hurried along the path, only pausing to assure he was still following the prints. At a certain point, he stopped, perplexed. There was only one Ruby-sized footprint now. He lowered to a crouch, studying the ground. Two holes were poked into the ground beside the single print. He looked ahead, noting that the pattern continued: one footprint, two narrow holes on each side. Then realization struck. Ruby was using sticks as crutches. His heart swelled so fiercely it ached.

This strong, brilliant woman…

She was being hunted in the woods, her ankle sprained, facing slick, rocky terrain, and she'd devised a solution on the fly. She was a genius. The bravest, most beautiful genius he'd ever met, and when he finally found her, he was going to gather her up into his arms and never let go.

He raced along the trail she'd left behind, the wind screaming and the rain pouring down like a wrath from Heaven. Lightning streaked across the sky, followed by deafening booms that shook the earth. Where was she? She couldn't have gone far, limping on her makeshift crutches.

Suddenly, a man's voice carried over the ruckus of the storm, singsong and cloying. Dex froze and strained to hear over the pelting rain.

"... I know you're close. Come out and see me."

Dex stiffened, searing-hot fury flooding him. This man had abducted Ruby, hurt her, and hunted her like prey. Now he was toying with her?

The coward expected to find a terrified, injured woman, alone and hiding in the woods.

What he wasn't expecting was a large, armed, former marine who was seriously ticked off.

Knowing he was nearly to the location Ruby had pinned, he pulled out his phone. He studied the map she'd sent, then scanned the woods around him. She was about fifty yards east of where he stood.

His heartbeat accelerated as he took off like a bullet out of a chamber, pushing past the dense foliage, paying no mind to the spiky branches slapping him in the face. Silently, he prayed that her pursuer hadn't caught up with her and that she was still there, tucked away safe in a hiding spot.

He reached the location indicated on the map and skidded to a halt. He scanned the trees, peering through the curtain of rain obscuring his view, his body thrumming with desperate hope. *Please be here.*

"Dex," Ruby whispered, her voice high with fear, and he'd never heard anything more beautiful in his life.

He ran toward the sound, his heart beating so wildly he thought it might explode. Her head of dark curls popped out from behind a thicket, dripping wet around her shoulders. She crawled toward him on her hands and knees, and his heart cracked wide open. These animals had reduced her to this: hurt, bleeding, and terrified, crawling through the mud to reach him.

He rushed to her, his throat choked with rage. He would hunt down the people doing this to her, and he wouldn't relent until they were behind bars. She looked up at him, her face bruised, tears streaking down her cheeks caked with mud. But her eyes…they were just as defiant as ever. Wide and bright and fiery. It was that fire inside her that had kept her alive.

He dropped to his knees in front of her, his heart aching. "It's okay, Killer. I've got you." He wrapped his arms around her, and she felt so small and vulnerable, shivering in her soaking-wet clothes.

"Dex, thank God," she breathed. She wiggled out of his grasp though, urgency in her movements. "The man's still out here. He's tracking me—"

A heavy weight smashed into Dex from behind, and he was shoved violently forward, the Glock flying out of his hand. He flipped onto his back to find himself face-to-face with Ruby's attacker. The man swung at his cheek, but Dex rolled, dodging the punch. He sprang up and reached for the Winchester slung across his back, but the man swept his feet out from under him. He caught himself before he fell, though, bending his knees and planting his feet firmly on the ground. He sent a forceful kick crashing into the man's ribs, and the guy rolled onto his side, groaning. Dex took a step toward Ruby, but the man grasped his foot and twisted it, sending him staggering back.

This guy had some training, and it showed. But Dex was

bigger, and he had the Lord on his side. The man jumped to his feet and rushed him, but Dex pivoted to the side, and the man crashed headfirst into a tree trunk. He dropped to the ground, wheezing in pain, and landed on his belly. He lay splayed out on the wet earth, his arms stretched in front of him.

"Dex, the Glock!" Ruby shouted.

Dex saw, but too late.

The man gripped the gun Dex had dropped, then grabbed Ruby with his other hand. He hauled her toward him, dragging her through the mud, and pressed the barrel to her forehead.

"Drop the rifle, or I shoot!" He yanked Ruby by the hair, and she yelped in pain.

Frustration boiled through Dex's veins, so hot he thought it would sear right through him. Then something flashed in Ruby's eyes. Not fear. A silent message. She was going to try something, and she was telling him to be ready.

Oh, he would be.

"I said, drop the rifle!" the man shrieked.

Fast as a streak of lightning, Ruby bit his hand and slipped out of his grasp.

Dex launched himself at him.

He rained down punches, pummeling the man with both fists. Somehow, through the fog of his fury, Ruby's voice carried to him.

"Dex." Her voice sounded strained, like she was in pain, but determined. "He's unconscious. You need to stop."

He paused and looked over at her, his body still brimming with anger toward the man who'd hurt her.

She was curled up in a ball, her expression drawn with pain. "We need to get out of here."

The need for vengeance was still bubbling in his veins,

but he obeyed. He would have liked to work this guy over until his searing-hot anger cooled, but that wasn't the man Dex was. At least, it wasn't the man God wanted him to be. With a shuddering breath, he looked down at the criminal lying on the ground and pulled out his phone.

"Are you going to call Reyes?" Ruby's voice was barely a murmur over the rush of the rain.

"Sort of." He forwarded their pinned location to the sheriff with a message.

Perp is here. Taking Ruby to a safe location.

Ruby glanced warily from her unconscious attacker to Dex. "Are the police on their way?"

"No doubt, but we'll be gone by the time they get here."

Her brow creased in confusion. "What do you mean? Where are we going?"

He wanted to answer her, but he wasn't sure how she would react. "I wish I had something to tie him up with until Reyes gets here."

Ruby scrunched up her eyebrows in thought, then her expression illuminated. "I have something."

She dug around in her pocket and produced a set of zip ties.

The same ones the monster had locked around her wrists. And they weren't even cut, but still intact.

A chuckle bubbled up in Dex's throat, inappropriate but irresistible. "How did you get them off?"

"A hairpin," she said casually, as if she weren't the most impressive, resourceful woman on the planet.

Dex shook his head, pride and wonder swelling in his soul. "Pass them over."

She did as he asked, her dirty, scratched-up fingers brushing his palm. Tenderness flooded him as he tucked the Glock back into his holster and then bound her attacker's hands. Then he strode over to her and scooped her up into his arms.

She was dripping wet, smeared with dirt and blood, and yet he'd never held anything so precious in his arms. He took off through the woods toward the crashed ATV, his plan already formed in his mind. He knew the one place he could take her where no one would think to look.

Where they would be safe.

He felt her gaze on him and looked down at her. She was studying him, her expression tense in concentration.

"Is Oliver okay?"

A pit opened in his stomach. Now that the threat was over, she was processing what had happened. All the terrible violence. "Yes. He was unharmed, and Nate is with him." He scanned her bruised, beautiful face. "Are you all right?" he asked thickly.

She pressed her lips together, never turning her eyes from his, and slowly nodded.

He snuggled her in closer. She felt so good curled against him, like she fit just right against his heart. Like he wanted to hold her there forever. When he spoke, his voice came out rough with emotion. "I would do anything to protect you."

She tucked her wet, curly head into the crook of his neck, her cheek cool and slick against his skin. "I'm starting to realize that."

NINE

Ruby looked up at the man carrying her through the woods, the man who'd risked his life to save her, again and again. Since her mother's death, she'd been on her own. A couple distant relatives, a few work friends, but she'd never let anyone get close—for her safety and theirs. She'd been a scrappy lone wolf since the age of seventeen.

She'd been so strong for so long. And honestly, it felt good to fall apart for once, knowing there was someone she trusted enough to put her back together.

The person who had offered her a job and a home when she'd been lost and alone. The person who had always protected her, even when she wouldn't let him. The person who would carry her when she was too broken to stand on her own two feet.

She took in the determined set of his jaw, the intensity burning in his ice-blue eyes, and the careful way he held her, like she was this beautiful gift he cherished. *God, I don't know what I did to deserve this man, but I thank You from the depths of my soul for placing him in my life.*

The rain had slowed to a drizzle, and through a clearing in the trees, she spied the ATV toppled on its side. They were back already? It had taken her an eternity to reach her hiding spot in the woods. Of course, she'd been limping on crutches made from sticks, and Dex was quickly covering the distance in his long, purposeful strides.

Skinny stood a bit farther down the trail, munching happily on some grass, and Ruby's earlier suspicions resurfaced.

"You had to ride Skinny out here to get me?"

Dex's eyes flickered with anger. "The tires on all the other ATVs were slashed."

Dread settled in her chest, cold and heavy. "This was a well-planned attack."

"An attack that failed." Dex's tone was hard and cold. He swept his gaze over her face, his expression feral. "Just like anything else they might try. I will not let them hurt you, Ruby."

He stopped a few feet away from the ATV and looked down at her, concern tensing his handsome features. "I need to set you down for a minute. Hold on to me for support."

He slid her down slowly, and she rested her hands on his shoulders. He unbuttoned the flannel over his T-shirt, slid it off, and draped it over the ground. Gently, he scooped her up and lowered her onto it.

"I need two hands to flip the ATV back over."

Her heart collapsed, and she looked up at him incredulously. "I'm already soaking wet and covered in mud. You didn't have to sacrifice your shirt for me."

He dropped to a crouch in front of her, his pale blue eyes sweeping over her face. "I won't set you down on the dirty ground, ever. And in case you hadn't already guessed, I would sacrifice anything for you."

Her heart stuttered as he stood and strode over to the ATV. She watched him angle his body like a lever and push up on the handlebars, feeling about as helpful as a tree stump. He grunted, his boots sliding in the mud, but the vehicle quickly righted. He tried the ignition switch, and it growled to life, thank the Lord.

He lifted her effortlessly and set her on the vehicle, then climbed on behind her.

"What about Skinny?" She registered the welcome warmth of his torso pressed to her back.

"I'll let one of the ranch hands know he's out here. They'll come get him once Reyes deals with your attacker."

Dex curled an arm around her waist and swept her dripping hair over her shoulder. "It's all going to be okay," he murmured, so warm and gentle and close. "I've got you." Without another word, he twisted the throttle and shot them down the trail.

She turned to look at him. "Don't you want to head the other direction?" Sitting this close, her voice carried over the sound of the engine. "We're going deeper into the woods, farther away from the ranch."

He pressed his lips together, keeping his eyes trained ahead. "I think it would be better if we...kept our distance for a while."

He was worried about the integrity of the sheriff's department. Ruby sensed that he trusted Reyes—she did, too—but if Walters had managed to manipulate Deputy Lewis, maybe he'd corrupted some of the other deputies. Her abductors had slid right through the sheriff's protection detail. Had it been an oversight, or a collaboration?

"I agree. But where can we go?" They were both soaked to the bone and needed shelter, and they had no supplies.

An exposed root jolted the ATV, and she leaned into him for support. His heart pounded against her back, and he snuggled her closer. Apparently, he had no trouble steering with one hand, since he'd grown up riding ATVs through these woods.

"There's a cabin farther out on my property. No one knows about it."

Her brows shot up. "A secret cabin?" She'd lived here for four months, driving cattle, and she'd never seen it.

He chuckled. "Yeah, I guess so."

"But what about Oliver?"

Dex slid his hand over hers, still holding her tight. "Even with everything you're going through right now, you're thinking of Oliver?"

"Of course I am! He needs someone to look after him."

Dex rested his cheek against hers, his skin impossibly warm. "That little guy's blessed to have you."

Butterflies swarmed in her belly, and she let her eyes flutter closed, relishing in his closeness.

"I'll ask Nate to take him back to his family's house tonight. He spends the night there from time to time and plays with Nate's younger siblings, so it will feel normal for him."

"And we'll call to check on him."

"Of course we will." He traced his thumb in a slow circle over her palm, eliciting even more butterflies. "Are you okay staying with me?" The low rumble of his voice vibrated through her. "I know it's…just the two of us. If you'd rather me take you somewhere else—"

"I'm okay with that." And she was. One hundred percent. She trusted this man like she'd never trusted anyone in her life. She relaxed against him, basking in his blissful heat. "You're like an oven."

He chuckled, and his low, smooth voice rumbled against her cheek again. It was the most pleasant feeling on earth.

"Most guys are."

She held her breath for a moment, feeling suddenly self-conscious. "Thank you for coming for me."

The words came out in a whisper, but sitting this close,

he heard. His chest caved against her, like all the air had whooshed out of it. Slowly, he lifted her hand to his mouth and brushed his lips over each of her fingertips.

"I always will."

Ruby closed her eyes and sank into the comfort of those words. Jude Dexler, her stubborn, overprotective boss, always shielding her from the other ranch hands, insisting on rushing to her rescue, even if it meant enduring her wrath afterward.

And she'd grown to *love* it.

He turned onto a narrow, bumpy trail she'd never seen before, leading them into a densely forested corner of his property. They kept going and going, until Ruby was about to ask if they were lost, when a small, simple cabin emerged among the trees. Dex parked the ATV beside it, lifted her into his arms again, and headed for the door.

She sighed with frustration. "I feel about as useful as a sack of potatoes."

He cradled her closer. "But you're *my* sack of potatoes."

She couldn't help it; a laugh bubbled up in her throat. She was filthy, bruised, and bleeding, and yet he was teasing her. And she *liked* it. She shook her head, defeated.

He shifted her into one arm and used the other to press a code into a keypad beside the door.

Ruby lifted a brow. "A *high-tech* secret cabin."

"I was always forgetting the key at the lodge, so I installed it last year." He pushed open the door to reveal a one-room cabin, spare but cozy, with a tiny kitchenette, a sofa, a bed and a wood-burning stove in the corner. Thick, lacquered beams stretched across the ceiling, and a door in the back probably—hopefully—led to a bathroom.

"I love it." Ruby noticed he'd still not made a move to release her. Probably because there wasn't a single surface he could set her on, filthy as she was. Of course, as far as she was concerned, he could take his time. "Do you come here often?"

"Used to." He headed for what was hopefully the bathroom door in the back. "My dad and I built this cabin when I was twelve. We used to hunt out here and stay overnight, just the two of us. Those were some of my best memories as a kid."

"And now you're too busy to use it because you're running the ranch?"

He nodded. "And rescuing beautiful women."

Ruby grinned. "Oh, beautiful women *plural*?"

He tossed her a boyish grin. Dex was handsome when he was gruff and brooding. When he was playful, he was devastating. "Nah, just one in particular."

He toed the door open with his boot and carried her into the compact bathroom. "All right, Killer." He set her gently on the edge of the bathtub. "Let's have a look at that ankle."

He knelt in front of her and gingerly propped her muddy shoe on his knee. She winced as he removed it, the fabric straining over the swollen joint. He slipped his fingers under the edge of her sock to slide it down, but she jerked her foot away, cheeks burning.

"I'm, ah, really gross right now. You can look at it after I've taken a shower."

His lips tipped up. "Ruby, I don't care about that."

She would care when he peeled off her wet sock to find a sweaty, mangled foot caked in dirt. He'd seen her dusty and disheveled out on the ranch, but this took dirty to a whole new level.

"After my shower," she said firmly.

His grin widened. "Yes, ma'am." He gently traced his fingers over her ruined ankle, his callused skin rasping over the fabric of her sock, and her pulse skittered through her veins. "Does anything else hurt?"

Everything else hurt. "Just some bumps and bruises."

His expression was doubtful, but he didn't press. "Think you can handle the shower all right?"

"Yeah." She would need to stand on one leg, but her balance was strong and her will was even stronger. She would take a hot shower if she needed to stand on her head to do it. "Too bad I'll have to put these dirty, wet clothes back on."

He gingerly lowered her foot to the floor. "I've got a few changes of clothes I keep here, and you're welcome to them, if you don't mind swimming in clothes twice your size."

Relief flooded her. Clean, dry clothes! "I'll take anything you have. Thank you." She was hardly in a position to be picky. She was prepared to wrap herself in a tablecloth if it meant never touching these wet, sticky clothes again.

He stood, rooted around in the cabinet beside the sink and pulled out a medicine bottle. "For the pain and swelling." He took her hand in his and shook two pills into her palm. Standing this close, his eyes blazed into hers. "I'll get you some water."

She stared after him, her heart coiled tight, until he returned a moment later. He placed a glass of water, a towel and a set of clean clothes on the vanity counter. "I'll call Nate and see how Oliver's doing."

"Let me know what he says."

Dex brushed a wet curl from her cheek and grinned. "Sure thing." He stepped out and shut the door behind him.

She closed her eyes, her heart full to the brim. *Lord, only You could make a man this gorgeous* and *thoughtful.*

After a hot shower, she felt human again, even though she'd needed to stand on one leg like a flamingo during the process. Dex's T-shirt fell almost to her knees, and she'd rolled his shorts several times so they wouldn't slide down her waist, but the oversized clothes were blissfully clean and dry. As an added bonus, they smelled just like him—fresh and spicy—and she couldn't resist pressing her face into the fabric and breathing in deep.

Still perched on one foot, she opened the door and glanced out. It was hardly a long distance to cover from the bathroom to the couch, but it stretched before her like miles with her throbbing ankle.

Dex turned from where he stood looking out the front window, his Glock in his hand and his Winchester slung over his back. He'd said they would be safe here, but clearly he wasn't letting his guard down.

His gaze trailed over her, his lips tipping up. "You look cute." He sheathed his Glock. "Need a lift?"

Self-consciousness tingled through her. "If you don't mind?"

His grin widened, and he strode toward her and scooped her up. His face inches from hers, he dropped his voice low. "You've probably guessed that I don't mind at all."

Ruby's heart did its best to leap out of her chest as he carried her to the sofa and deposited her carefully on the cushions.

"How's Oliver?"

"Nate got him calmed down pretty quick. He was more worried about you than himself." Pride flickered in his eyes. "And Skinny's safe in his stall."

Relief sank into her bones. At least the little guy was far away from this mess. Far away from her, even though it made her heart hurt. "Thanks for checking."

He swallowed hard, and his eyes never left hers. "I take care of the people I care about. And that includes you, Ruby."

Her cheeks heated, and anticipation closed her throat up too tightly to talk.

"I know it's hard for you to accept help," he continued.

"I'm not sure why, since I don't know about your past." A tremor of hurt shook in his voice, then he went on. "But I'm hoping you'll let me."

This beautiful, generous man was begging to take care of her, as if she might refuse the offer? "Okay."

He brushed his fingers through her damp curls. "Okay."

And he did. Raiding the kitchen, he found ice, which he wrapped in a dishtowel to make a cold compress and canned peas and carrots from the cupboard to make her dinner. Beyond his gentle concern for her, Ruby didn't miss his frequent glances out the windows or the way his hand slid occasionally over his Glock.

After cleaning up, he lowered himself onto the end of the couch where she was currently sprawled, her stomach full and her eyes drooping.

He propped her foot on his lap and swept his gaze over her. "Those painkillers kicking in?"

She nodded with a sleepy smile. He massaged her calf, the soothing caress making her even drowsier. She looked up to find him watching her intently, his expression hard to read. She couldn't mistake the affection she saw there—Dex's feelings for her had developed into something much deeper than boss and employee. Deeper than friends. But there was a wariness in his eyes, like he was holding back a part of him. A part she desperately wanted to claim as her own.

His trust.

But how could she blame him, when she'd been hiding her true self from him these last four months? Even now, when he was moving heaven and earth to protect her.

Maybe it was time to change that. Time to trust him with her most vulnerable secrets.

Lord, give me the courage.

Her pulse raced with fear, but she forced herself to stop thinking and just speak from her heart.

"My mother was murdered when I was seventeen."

Dex's gaze sharpened, and his body went rigid. "Ruby… I'm so sorry." His eyes locked on hers, waiting patiently for her to continue.

"She was an investigative reporter who'd uncovered damning evidence against a very powerful man. He had our house set on fire. I escaped." Her voice dropped to a murmur. "My mom didn't."

His breath caught, and he leaned over her protectively, as if he could shield her from the pain in her past.

"This man had the influence to block any investigation against him," she continued. "But I wanted justice for my mom, and I wanted to prevent him from hurting anyone ever again. So I joined the FBI and went undercover to collect evidence against him."

Dex's eyes widened. "You're an FBI agent?"

She nodded.

"That explains a lot." His lips curved up.

Silence blanketed the room as he processed everything. "This evidence…" he finally said. "Do you have it?"

She lifted her chin. "Yes."

Pride shone in his eyes, and his hands tightened around her. "You are…" He swallowed hard. "The most incredible person I've ever met."

Tears welled in her eyes. His praise and his faith in her overwhelmed her soul. "What I know will destroy him. That's why he's so desperate to silence me."

Dex leaned forward, his eyes blazing. "This powerful man. Who is he?"

Here it was. The point of no return. She sucked in a deep breath, holding his stare. "Senator Jim Walters."

Dex's jaw dropped. Clearly, he'd heard about the high-profile scandal, since it had been splashed over the media. Was he going to dismiss her, like everyone else had when her mom died? She sank her teeth into her bottom lip and held her breath. Dex believing her shouldn't matter, but it did.

When he spoke, his tone was fierce. "I won't let him touch you, Ruby. I won't let him anywhere near you until you're in that courtroom, delivering him the justice he deserves."

All the air left her lungs. He believed her. Of course he did. Dex had been there for her since the first moment. She sat up, reached out her hand, and ran it through his hair. He squeezed his eyes shut and pulled her palm to his mouth, covering it in kisses.

"Ruby…" He blinked his eyes open to gaze at her through those glittering, incandescent blue irises.

Her heart melted at the raw emotion she saw shining back at her. "There's…one more thing." She swallowed hard, gathering her courage. "My name is Isadora."

The tension in his posture, the wary glint in his eyes, every remaining scrap of restraint dissipated, and he pulled her into his arms.

"Isadora." Her real name on his lips spread warmth through her soul, like the feeling of finally coming home after a very long journey. His mouth was so close to hers, their lips nearly touched as he spoke. "Can I kiss you?"

She threaded her fingers through his so-soft hair. "Please."

He brushed his lips against hers, the gentle contact like a tingle of electricity between them. She returned his kiss, and he deepened it, gently cradling the nape of her neck.

He pulled back a moment later and pressed his forehead to hers. "You have no idea how long I've wanted to do that."

She curled her arms around him, her soul swimming in warm, shimmery happiness. "How long?"

He traced the curve of her jaw with his thumb. "Since the moment you showed up at my ranch, too little for your big attitude."

She let out a laugh. "Really? You always seemed so… brooding."

His expression turned sober, and his thumb paused on its path down the slope of her neck. "I had trouble trusting because of my…past." He looked deeply into her eyes, his expression open and sincere. "But you came into my life, shining through all that darkness."

Isadora's heart stuttered. "I'm so sorry, Dex. I hated lying to you."

He slid his hand up until it was buried in her curls. "You had to. I understand… Isadora."

A tide of warmth washed over her. "I love hearing you say my real name. I love that you finally know me."

His gaze roamed her face. "Even if I didn't know your name, I've known *you* since the first moment."

He kissed her again, slow and sweet, taking his time, like there wasn't danger pressing in from all sides. Like he could scatter all the shadows from her past, present, and future. For one blissful moment, he occupied every corner of her mind, overwhelmed all her senses, until there was only *him*.

He finally untangled his lips from hers and tucked an errant curl behind her ear. "You need to rest. I'll keep watch."

She wanted to protest, but her eyelids were like lead drooping over her eyes. She settled back on the couch. "Wake me up in a couple hours so you can sleep."

His lips tipped up in that boyish grin she loved so much. "Not happening." He planted a kiss on her forehead and rose. "Sleep, Isadora. I've got you."

* * *

The woods were a pitch-black blanket wrapped around the cabin, the dark absolute out here in the middle of nowhere.

Such poor visibility didn't sit well with Dex as he kept watch from the cabin's front porch, his palm on his Glock and his Winchester across his back.

He checked Ruby—Isadora—regularly as she slept. He had to drag himself away; he could have watched her delicate features for hours. But at the moment, he didn't have the luxury of lingering.

It was after 10:00 p.m., and the air was cool with a lingering humidity from the earlier storm. All had been silent since they'd arrived, but that did nothing to calm his restless energy. The threat was out there somewhere, lurking in those ink-black woods, coiled and ready to strike—

An ear-splitting *crack* cleaved the air, shattering the silence of the night. Dex's Winchester was in his hands before he realized he'd reached for it, his instincts taking the helm.

The shot had originated from the woods straight ahead, about two hundred yards away. But how had these guys found his cabin? Of course, they were watching his property and knew he and Isadora hadn't returned to the lodge. And with the ground muddy from the rain, they could have followed their ATV tracks.

A surge of adrenaline flooded his muscles, urging him to run toward the source of the shot, but his logic pumped the brakes. If this ruthless senator pursuing Isadora had sent his assassins out here to kill her, they would take a stealthier approach than some sloppy shot from two hundred yards away.

Something was off. Maybe the shot was a distraction, an attempt to separate him from Isadora.

I will not leave your side again. His own words echoed through his mind, like a warning. No, he wouldn't take off half-cocked into the woods. He could only protect Isadora if he stayed close.

He pulled his phone out of his pocket and dialed Reyes. The sheriff picked up on the first ring.

"What's up?"

"Someone shot at the cabin on my property where we're staying. I'll text you the location."

He hadn't wanted the entire sheriff's department to know where they were, in case Senator Jim Walters tried to corrupt another deputy, but Dex needed backup, and he trusted his former marine friend with his life.

And Isadora's, which was much more precious.

He ended the call then texted Reyes a pin of their location. Another shot rang out, same direction, but closer this time. His heart hammered, and he lifted his rifle and peered through the sight. The moment a gunman came into view, he would be ready.

"Dex?" Isadora's voice carried from inside the cabin, pitched high with fear. "I heard gunshots."

Dex's anger flared, hot and bright. He'd promised her he would protect her, but her attackers kept coming, cold-blooded and unrelenting. They'd bruised and bloodied her and turned her life into a nightmare.

That stopped *now*.

He rushed back into the cabin, his blood boiling at the panic etched on her beautiful features, so peaceful in sleep just moments ago.

"Take this." He thrust his Glock into her hand. "But promise me you'll stay inside, okay?"

She was a trained field agent, savvy and tough, but she was injured right now, and he needed to keep her far away from this threat until police arrived.

Her expression was tense with fear. "Don't chase after

them, Dex. They're trying to lure you out to separate you from me."

"I know." So smart. So brilliant and beautiful. He locked eyes with her, the intensity of his feelings overwhelming him. "I won't leave you, Isadora. Ever." He turned for the door—just as the windows burst open in a spray of glass and multiple explosions ripped through the room.

"Isadora!" He lunged for her and covered her body with his. His eyes frantically scanned the room, assessing the source of the explosions. Multiple glass bottles littered the floor, burning furiously. Molotov cocktails. They'd thrown one into each window, four in the front—he craned his neck to study the back of the cabin—and two in the back.

The cabin was made entirely of wood, and with the stiff breeze blowing in from every window, fire would spread out of control in minutes. Bright, hot tongues of flame were already creeping up the walls, racing hungrily for the beams stretched across the ceiling, filling the tiny living room with smoke.

They needed to get out *now.*

He rushed to one of the windows, peered out the broken glass and his gut coiled into a tight knot. Three armed men materialized in the darkness, stepping out from the tree line, their guns aimed at the cabin.

Evacuating from the front would mean stepping into their death. He turned his gaze frantically to Isadora, who had risen on one foot, one palm pressed against the back of the couch for support, the other gripping the Glock.

Her intelligent eyes registered her understanding. "They're waiting for us out there, aren't they?"

He hated the fear in her voice. The desperation. "We'll go out the back," he shouted over the roar of the growing fire. "There's a rear door that leads outside."

She nodded and let him sweep her up in one arm, tucking her into his torso as he held the rifle ready in the other hand. They crossed the room and threw open the back door to find three more gunmen, spread out in a perimeter around the cabin, weapons trained on them.

Dex slammed the door shut and spun away, shielding Isadora with his body as bullets peppered the door. His heart jackhammered as his gaze collided with hers, her eyes wide with terror and disbelief.

"There's no way out," she breathed. Trembles racked her frame, and her voice came out thin as a thread. "We're trapped."

•

TEN

Isadora was thrust violently back to the age of seventeen, trapped in a burning house with her dying mother's desperate screams.

Radiant heat pressed in from all sides as hungry flames licked up the walls, consuming the wooden panels and fabric curtains. Already the small space was choked with smoke, and the temperature was climbing fast. Her skin tingled uncomfortably, and it wouldn't take long for the heat to become unbearable.

The burn scar on her calf flamed, searing her skin, and she needed to fight down her rising panic.

"We don't have much time," Dex shouted over the crackle of the flames.

He was right. An old log cabin like this provided about as much fire resistance as dry kindling. But her reactions were sluggish, her muscles like lead, and her head fuzzy like it was stuffed with cotton. It wasn't smoke inhalation—yet—but something deeply emotional dragging her down, pulling her under the surface like a riptide. Overwhelming. Inescapable.

"Isadora, go! Get out!"

It wasn't Dex's voice calling to her, but her mother's. Isadora hurtled back in time to the two-bedroom bungalow in the suburbs outside DC where she'd grown up. The air inside the living room was unbreathable. The heat unbearable. The first floor had collapsed into the living room, separating her from her mother. Trapping her.

"Go, Isadora!"

"No!" She couldn't even see her mother past the heavy smoke and angry red flames. But she heard her screams of agony as the fire consumed her.

Until she fell silent.

"Isadora, c'mon!"

Dex's voice this time. He pulled her to the floor, where the air was clearer, and led her to one of the broken windows.

"Take a breath!" He guided her to the hole smashed in the glass. "Then get back down."

She drank in deep gulps of clean, cool air, holding the last breath in her lungs.

Three gunshots cracked against the window frame, and she darted down, seized with panic. Dex dove on top of her, his heart pounding against her back, covering her until the gun fell silent.

Of course Walters's men would keep their guns trained on the windows and doors, trying to catch a shot at them. Denying them access to an exit or clean air.

Dex rolled onto his side, his face inches from hers, still gripping his rifle. "We need to take out all these guys so we can escape."

She'd counted six gunmen out there, and they would need to eliminate all of them before they were burned alive or shot through an open window.

But the cabin was growing hotter by the second, the air denser from smoke. And her mother's screams ripped through her memory…

"Isadora!" Dex's voice pierced the fog of her mind. His frenzied gaze raked over her face. "Are you okay?"

She nodded vigorously, trying to keep it together. She could not afford to fall apart right now.

"You take this window. I'll take a window on the other side." The blue irises of his eyes danced in the light of the fire, bright and intense. "We will survive this. I promise you."

He pressed his mouth roughly to hers, then rolled onto his belly and army-crawled to the window across the room. Only a few feet and a thin veil of smoke separated them, but she wanted to cry out for him to come back.

But his strategy was logical, and necessary. Gunmen surrounded the house. They'd be able to take them out faster if they split up.

Steeling her resolve, she chanced a quick peek out the window, locating one of the gunmen. Moving with a speed and accuracy she'd honed in her training, she aimed the barrel of her Glock and released two shots. The dark form of a man slumped to the ground, and she dove back below the window.

Isadora's heart leapt in triumph, even as guilt sliced through her. She'd shot another human being. Even though the man was trying to kill her, even though she had no choice, her respect for human life would not allow her to celebrate.

Lord, I pray I only wounded him.

Her body burned with the need for more air, but the thin wisps of smoke had thickened, and breathing that in would damage her lungs.

She popped up, took a deep pull of air from the broken window, and dropped just as shots exploded and shards of glass rained down on her head. She squeezed her eyes shut, praying silently as jagged pieces of glass lodged in her hair and clothing, cutting and slicing her skin. She nearly gasped but remembered to hold in her precious lungful of air. The one she'd nearly given her life for.

How much longer could she continue like this? The cabin

was moments away from collapse, and she and Dex would die of burns or smoke inhalation before they took out the remaining five gunmen.

Dex fired a shot out his window, glanced back at her, and nodded.

Make that four.

Focus, Isadora. Don't give up hope. Pulling the collar of her borrowed T-shirt over her nose and mouth, she belly-crawled to another smashed window in the back. Its curtains had not yet caught flame, and she hid behind them to take a peek outside. Her eyes stung and watered from the smoke, but she could just make out two more gunmen at two o'clock and four o'clock. Staying concealed, she nosed her Glock out the hole in the window and aimed. Two shots in quick succession.

Bang! Bang!

One man doubled over, grasping his trigger hand. The other took the hit straight to the shoulder. Hopefully that would take them out of the action for a while.

Another two shots rang out from the front of the cabin, where Dex was taking aim.

"One left!" he called, his voice rough with smoke.

She held up her hand and made a circular motion, hoping he would understand they needed to check all the windows to locate the one remaining gunman.

Through the haze, she saw Dex move to the next window, staying low, and then the next, briefly checking outside and—hopefully—taking a quick sip of air.

Isadora did the same. Her eyes burned as she checked each window, straining past the haze of smoke and tears to survey the pitch-black woods. The shooter could be anywhere, but under the cover of night, her only chance of spotting him was if he moved.

Either way, they couldn't stay there much longer. They

needed to flee the fire raging through the cabin before they asphyxiated or the structure collapsed, trapping them inside.

But if they left before they'd taken out the final gunman, they would step out into a barrage of bullets.

Despair and white-hot panic gripped her tight, closing off her throat, dizzying her. Making her teeter.

No, that was the lack of oxygen.

She needed to take a breath, even if that meant exposing herself for a moment.

She rose, took a quick sip of air from a window, and ducked back down.

A bullet sang past her ear, and despite the scalding heat, icy cold slipped down her spine.

As long as the final gunman was out there, they couldn't go out the door without risking being shot.

They needed to take him out. But they were running out of time. She squeezed her eyes shut against the burning, toxic air, fighting back the hysteria creeping into her thoughts…

Arms snaked around her, and she nearly jumped out of her skin, but she turned to find Dex.

She almost cried out his name, but she couldn't release her breath. Not yet, when it was still saturated with precious oxygen. Instead, she buried her face in his shirt, tears tracing a cool path down her scorched cheeks.

Dex held her a moment, then pulled away to take a breath from the window above them. A shot quickly followed, and he dove to the floor, pulling her down beneath him. He pressed his mouth to her ear and released his breath in one long, rushed sentence.

"I'll create a diversion go out the back I love you."

"No!" The word escaped her mouth, along with all the oxygen it carried. But she didn't care. She wouldn't let him do this. She reached out to grasp him, to pull him back, but he'd already crawled away.

"Dex!" Anything she might have said next was blocked by a fit of violent coughs, her lungs inflamed by smoke and heat and all the poisonous particles in the air.

Still, she crawled after him. She couldn't let him go out that front door. They may have taken out five of the gunmen, but it only took one person and one bullet to kill. And she would not allow Dex to sacrifice himself for her. She would not let a cold-blooded killer rip Dex from Oliver's life.

From her life.

Because she could no longer imagine life without him.

Frantic, Isadora squinted against the stinging haze separating her from Dex. The smoke was so thick now she couldn't see him on the other side of the small room. She sucked in a hiccupping sob between coughs, her lungs clogged with smoke, and nearly surrendered to despair. But she needed to press on. She could not allow him to open that door.

"Dex, stop!" she yelled, but only a strained rasp tore from her throat, not even audible over the roar of the flames. "Dex..."

A thunderous groan cleaved the air, reverberating through her body, and she jerked her head up in time to see a thick, wooden beam detach from the ceiling.

Lord, no...

It fell in what seemed like slow motion, sinking through the smoke like a knife slicing a living, breathing beast. The massive beam came crashing down in a riot of angry red sparks, shaking the tiny cabin with a thunderous *boom.*

Followed by a bellow of pain.

No! No, no, no...

She scrambled forward, ignoring the spasms in her chest and the darkness creeping into the edges of her vision. Somewhere in a back corner of her consciousness, she realized she was on the verge of passing out.

But reaching Dex was the priority.

Staying low, her face nearly pressed to the ground where the air was almost breathable, she slid on her stomach until she was as close to the blazing beam as she could tolerate. Through the thick smoke, she spotted Dex.

His leg was pinned under the beam.

He strained to lift the heavy wood off his body, where it pressed down on him just above the knee, but it hardly budged.

"Isadora, go!" he shouted, his voice hoarse and barely audible.

My God, I'm going to lose him.

Her mind sank deeper and deeper, like it was sucked down by a swirling vortex, back to the most horrible moment in her past...

Isadora, go! her mother was shouting. *Get out of the house!*

The collapsed first floor separated them, barring her mother from the exit.

Mom! she'd screamed, her voice younger, sharper, terrified. *Mom, no!*

Isadora was drowning, pulled down to the dark depths of those memories. She squeezed her eyes shut, struggling to kick back up to the surface, but she felt paralyzed. Scalding, hungry flames swirled around her—then and now—consuming everything in their path, pressing in on her. Hellish heat overwhelmed her, smoke dizzied her mind, and she couldn't move. Couldn't *think*.

Walters had ripped away the person she'd loved most in the world.

Now he was doing it again.

And she was so, so weary of fighting...

Just as her eyes began to droop, her gaze connected with Dex's. His last words had been so rushed, but she knew she hadn't misheard them.

I love you.

Somehow, those three words pierced the fog of her mind and lifted her soul above the smoke and the heat and the despair. She loved Dex, too. And she intended to tell him that. Right after she saved him.

Father, give me strength.

Determination swelled inside her.

"Isadora, please…get out," Dex rasped, his voice growing weaker. "I'm…right behind you."

Not. Happening.

She drilled her gaze into his and spoke between hacking coughs. "Give me…your rifle."

His brow furrowed, but he pulled the weapon off his shoulder and slid it under the beam separating them. The searing-hot metal burned her skin, but she quickly slid her palm over the wooden grip.

She thrust the rifle barrel under the beam, gripped the other end in her hand, and pushed up as hard as she could, using the rifle as a lever.

Dex's eyes flashed with understanding. He sat up and pushed with both hands, working in tandem with her. The beam budged slightly, but it wasn't enough for Dex to slide his leg out.

She could have screamed with frustration. She couldn't imagine the pain he was in right now, crushed by the enormous weight of that wood.

She adjusted the angle of the rifle, praying it wouldn't snap under pressure. The beam budged even more.

"It's working!" she cried, her voice a scratchy croak.

Dex redoubled his efforts, his muscles bulging and the

veins popping in his neck. He was fighting for his life. For her life, too, because she refused to leave him there.

The beam lifted another inch.

It was enough.

Dex yanked his leg free and sprang to his feet, leaping over the beam to reach her.

Isadora watched him, eyes wide despite the stinging smoke. There was no way his leg wasn't injured, crushed beneath the weight of that beam. He must have been moving on pure adrenaline.

Suddenly, his arms were around her, crushing her into his chest. He skimmed his hands over her, tense and shaking.

"Are you hurt? Can you breathe?"

"I'm okay," she rasped. She really wasn't. Spasms had overtaken her lungs, rejecting the burning, sooty air she was forcing into them. "We need…to go."

He pointed to the back door. "Go ahead of me."

She dropped to her belly and dragged herself forward with her forearms. Even the ground was hot now, scalding her skin like burning-hot sand on a beach. Her arms and legs felt raw and covered in blisters, her old burn scar blazing with pain, but she had no choice but to keep moving forward, never pausing, even when hacking coughs shook her body. Dex was right behind her, and the back door was only a few feet away. A few feet from cool, fresh air. Her lungs were burning and begging for it.

But the fresh, life-giving air would bring deadly bullets with it.

These could be the last breaths they took.

They reached the door, and she turned to Dex. "We need… a plan."

He sat up and propped his back against the wall, his chest

heaving. He'd recovered his rifle and was holding it in both hands. "I'll go first and take out the shooter—"

"I meant a plan that…doesn't involve you dying."

She didn't know how many bullets remained in his Winchester, but her Glock's magazine only had three left. Not enough to properly cover him if he ran out that door. But staying even a moment longer in this cabin was not an option. She was dizzy with lack of oxygen, coughing uncontrollably, and the darkness creeping into the edges of her vision had blotted out everything but a narrow tunnel of light.

She was a few missed breaths away from passing out.

They could run out the door at the same time, but with her mangled ankle…

The door banged open, making the decision for them. A rush of cool, clean air swept past her face, and her lungs expanded, drinking it in.

Just as an armed man burst through the door.

Before she could react, Dex rushed him, hitting him low in the gut and tackling him to the ground. They rolled outside onto the grass, Dex landing on top and raining punches like hellfire on the guy's face. They'd both dropped their guns in the scuffle, but she still held her Glock firmly in her hand. This was her chance. She crawled out onto the grass just as another man stepped in front of her, blocking her path.

Walters.

She scurried back, her eyes wide with disbelief. He was *here*, waiting outside the burning home, just like that night ten years ago. Making sure the job was done right.

Fury flashed in his glare, his lips turned up in a vicious snarl. "No guns for you, Isadora."

With a quick swipe of his foot, he kicked the Glock out of her hands. It landed several feet away, out of reach, and her throat tightened with despair.

He grabbed her by the front of her shirt and hauled her onto her feet. Sharp blades of agony shot up her ankle, the pain so intense she nearly lost consciousness. Walters looked down, his shrewd eyes alight with interest. "Aw, did you hurt yourself?" he taunted. He splayed both hands over her shoulders and pushed her—forcing her back toward the hellish blaze pouring out of the cabin. "Don't worry. It's a short walk."

No! God, no... She resisted, but he was stunningly strong. In his mid-fifties and muscular, Senator Jim Walters was publicly known for his campaigns for health and fitness. He regularly posted about his training routines.

She felt that strength right now—shoving her into the hell she'd just escaped. She stumbled backward, limping, the pain in her ankle excruciating. She'd inhaled too much smoke, and her muscles felt like lead, unresponsive to her brain's commands. She shot a frantic look at Dex, who was sparring with the gunman on the lawn. His gaze landed on her and he took a step toward her, but the man yanked him back, landing a punch to his jaw.

Dex's head snapped to the side, and Isadora gasped. "Dex!"

"I'm coming," he yelled, but the other man swung again, landing another punch while Dex was distracted.

Her pulse raced with terror. *Father, protect him.* Dex couldn't help her right now. That meant she needed to face Walters on her own.

"I'm disappointed in you." Walters's mocking tone snagged her attention back to him. He pressed his face close to hers, his features demonic in the firelight. "You're supposed to be this trained field agent, and I'm pushing you around like a rag doll. You're no stronger than you were at seventeen."

She clenched her jaw and pushed back, sweat pouring down her face from the effort, as well as the overwhelming heat pouring off the cabin. A coughing fit seized her as

Walters gripped her under her arms and half dragged, half carried her toward the billowing black smoke pouring from the open door.

The roaring flames behind her had only gathered strength since she'd left. The space where she and Dex had hunkered by the door was now a raging ball of fire. If Walters managed to push her back in, she would be dead in an instant.

"You're just like your mother." His eyes gleamed with evil. "You like to play with fire."

Raw, unfettered rage screamed through her veins. She would *not* let him push her into that cabin. And she would not let his violence toward her mother or anyone else go unpunished.

"You won't testify against me," Walters continued, his voice rough with the effort of shoving her backward. "Just like your mom never published her investigation into my… business." He cocked his head to the side, as if amused. "Funny how you're going to die just like she did. Burned by her own self-righteous battle for justice. You've both done this to yourselves."

Was this how he justified his actions? By blaming his victims to absolve himself?

She shot a panicked glance at Dex, who was still struggling to free himself from their other attacker.

Lord, please come to his aid...and mine.

The fire scorched her back, where she now stood only a couple feet away from the hungry tongues of flame. Her coughing had worsened, too, so she was barely sucking in breaths between spasms. And her body was so, so heavy…

"It's time to give up now, little Isadora." Walters's face twisted into an expression of maniacal glee. He was ending her life to keep her from testifying, but he was enjoying it, too. The sadistic gleam in his eyes confirmed it. "You've spent the last ten years trying to beat me, only to end up a charred lump, just like your mother. How pathetic."

He gave her one final shove, meant to send her stumbling into the fire, but she dropped to her knees, lowering her center of gravity, and hunched down. Her muscles trembled and ached, heavy like stone, but that fire inside her simply would not give in.

Lord, if it is Your will, fight this battle beside me.

She scanned the ground, searching for a dropped weapon. There, in the grass. Dex's Winchester. How many bullets did it have left? She had no idea, but it was her only chance.

Walters scowled, clearly annoyed that he had to work so hard to kill her. He bent down and gripped her roughly by the shoulders, fury etched in his features.

Now.

Gathering the last ounce of her strength, she thrust out her elbow, sending it crashing into his nose. He roared in pain, and for a moment, loosened his grip.

Move, Isadora!

Dragging her leaden body as fast as she could, she lunged for the rifle, rolled onto her back, and pulled the trigger. An explosive *crack* left the chamber.

Walters dodged and was on her in a second flat.

He knelt over her, using his brute strength to pin down her hands. She twisted, pushed, and kicked, fighting desperately to free her hand long enough to squeeze off another shot.

Bracing herself, she smashed her forehead into his. He froze, dazed for a moment, and she aimed, pulled the trigger…

Nothing.

She was out of bullets.

She let out a rasping scream of despair. There was no time to search for another gun. No time to wait for Dex's help. And she wasn't strong enough to push Walters off.

The senator looked at the gun, then at her, and laughed.

Laughed.

The monster who'd killed her mother. Who'd tried to kidnap Oliver and burn her and Dex alive in that cabin. He'd targeted every person she'd ever loved, and now he was laughing in her face.

Her body started to tremble. A wave of raw, intense emotion washed over her, and she cocked the Winchester back and swung it like a baseball bat right into Walters's skull.

His eyes lost focus and his mouth popped open in shock.

Then he crumpled to the ground, out cold.

"Isadora!"

Dex rushed toward her, his opponent sprawled across the lawn, and her eyes welled with tears of relief. Dex was okay. So was she.

Lord, thank You.

Her arms wobbly, she crawled to him on all fours. He scooped her up and pulled her into a fierce embrace. He held a gun in one hand, which he must have recovered from the other man. He trained it on their two attackers lying on the ground, in case they had the very bad idea of waking up.

He raked his gaze over her, his eyes wild with worry. "Are you all right? Did he hurt you?"

"He didn't..." A fit of coughing seized her, and she waited until it passed. "He didn't hurt me."

Dex lifted her up against him, taking the weight off her ankle. He pressed his lips to her sweaty, ash-covered forehead and stroked her hair. "Thank God."

She brushed her fingertips over his face, examining the bruises already forming in the light of the blaze behind them. "How's your leg?"

He waved away her concern. "Not broken."

She imagined it hurt like crazy, and it would feel even

worse once the adrenaline wore off. But, thankfully, he didn't seem seriously injured.

He pressed his forehead to hers, so their lips lightly touched when he spoke. "You refused to walk away from me, back there in the cabin." His eyes blazed into hers. "You saved my life, Isadora. You are the bravest, most incredible person I've ever met."

Her heart floated up into her throat, and tears stung her eyes. "Dex."

He brushed his lips over hers. "In case you didn't catch what I said back there in the cabin—we were a little busy at the time—" His mouth tipped up in that boyish grin. "I love you."

Fresh tears filled her eyes, her heart so full she thought it would burst. "I love you, Jude Dexler. I love you so much."

She pressed her mouth to his, and he kissed her deeply, with all the wild emotion building over the last four days.

With all the love that had grown between them over the last four months.

The rumble of engines vibrated the air, and they turned to see three ATVs surge out of the woods.

Reyes and three of his deputies.

Their headlights flooded the lawn, revealing Walters and the other assailants sprawled on the grass.

The deputies charged toward them and, even though they were already incapacitated, pinned them to the ground and cuffed them. Walters cracked open his eyelids and locked gazes with Isadora, his expression crazed with fear and astonishment.

"See you in court," she called out to him as police dragged him away.

Dex let out a low chuckle and turned her to face him. "So brave," he murmured, the cabin's flames dancing in his eyes.

He holstered the gun he'd held trained on their attackers and enveloped her in his arms.

She relaxed against him, her adrenaline washing away in a tide of relief.

And deep, overwhelming fatigue. She forced in a rasping breath, her heavy eyelids drooping over her stinging eyes. She'd inhaled a lot of smoke, and now that the fight-or-flight response had ebbed away, her body was throwing in the towel.

Dex's expression sharpened, and he called out to Reyes, who was directing the other deputies. "We need an ambulance at the ranch. I'm taking her back now."

Reyes spoke into a radio, then turned back to Dex. "On the way. Take care of her."

"I intend to." His arms tightened around her. "Ready to get out of here?"

She gave him a sleepy grin, her eyes half closed. "*So* ready."

He lifted her and carried her to his ATV parked in front of the cabin. She was deposited carefully on the seat, then felt him climb on behind her. He swept her hair to the side and pressed a kiss to her neck, sending happy shivers through her. "The nightmare is over now. You're safe."

A wracking sob shook her body. It was really over: the years of fear and pain and living a double life. She still needed to testify, but Walters had been caught red-handed. She would reach out to her boss at the Bureau to coordinate with Reyes and ensure Walters stayed in police custody.

That meant she was free.

Despite the heaviness of her fatigue, her spirit soared.

Dex's lips brushed her neck as he spoke. "I'm going to take care of you, Isadora. Always, if you like."

Always?

Her pulse accelerated, and she turned to find his expression was so earnest it made her heart ache. She slipped her arms around his neck and smiled. “Always sounds perfect to me.”

His handsome face split into a wide grin, and he twisted the throttle on the ATV. “Let’s go start forever, then.”

EPILOGUE

Ten months later

"C'mon, Isadora!" Oliver bounded toward her, his silky, little-boy hair bouncing in the sunshine. "Let's go see the new calves!"

Isadora set her sack of grass seed on the ground, wiped her hands down the front of her jeans, and turned to grin at the little guy.

"Let's go, let's go!" He pulled on her hand. "Nate said they were just born last night!"

Spring was a busy time on a cattle ranch. She'd been reseeding an overgrazed area of pasture all morning while Dex surveyed his fencing, making needed repairs. His parents had even flown in to help for a few weeks. It was a lively, bustling, joyful time of renewal; calves were born, nature was blooming, and the sprawling, verdant property was buzzing with new life and hope.

And Isadora's life was on a path of renewal as well.

During the long, high-profile trial in DC, Dex had stayed by her side. His dad, John, and mom, Dawn, had flown back from Arizona to run the ranch in his absence. Dex's calm, supportive presence had lent her strength during the fear and uncertainty of that time. Not to mention, the prosecution had required his statement as well, as a witness of the attempted murder at his cabin. It had been a dark time, but they'd walked the path together in the light of the Lord, supporting each other.

Ultimately, Isadora's testimony against Senator Jim Walters had landed him in prison for life for the murder of Rebecca de la Cruz, as well as fraud and unauthorized disclosure of classified information. Several of Walters's cronies were facing justice as well, including Greg Ward, Isadora's witness security inspector, who had been charged with accepting bribes from the senator in exchange for his cooperation. Isadora was now a superstar among the intelligence community, and the FBI had begged her to stay.

Yet, here she was, planting seed in a pasture, spending her days in the rugged beauty of the Montana countryside—with the little boy and handsome cowboy who had stolen her heart.

Choosing between the loves of her life and the Federal Bureau of Investigation? Easy call.

Oliver danced impatient circles around her. "C'mon, Isadora! C'mon, c'mon, c'mon."

She chuckled. "Okay, Ollie Man. You know, those calves aren't going anywhere in the next five minutes."

He ignored this, pulling her across the yard to the barn. He was still living on the ranch, but his mom, Devon, was back in his life, cleaning herself up, and visiting Oliver regularly. The little guy was thrilled, and so were Isadora and Dex.

They visited the pens of the newborn calves, Oliver convincing Nate to let him pet them, clean their stalls, and do their health checks. Nate was great with the little guy, explaining everything patiently and letting him help.

"Looks like we have a little rancher in training." Dex's arms looped around Isadora's waist, and she turned to him, her pulse quickening.

Yeah, it still did that every time.

"Can I steal one of your helpers here, Nate?"

Nate chuckled. "You're the boss."

Dex pressed a kiss to her temple. "Come for a ride with me?"

The low timbre of his voice flowed through her like warm honey, and she slid her hand into his. "Sure."

He led her to Moody and Skinny, already saddled, and they climbed up and headed out across the pasture.

"Where are we going?"

Dex rode beside her, those sky-blue eyes settling on hers. "Your favorite spot."

The glade. A grassy patch of meadow nestled in the mountains, about a fifteen-minute ride from the ranch. She'd spent hours there last fall, after the trial, reveling in its peace and beauty after the long, ugly ordeal with Walters. With the busyness of the spring rush, she hadn't had a chance to visit it in weeks. By now, it would be blooming with wildflowers.

Her gaze snagged on Dex, and her heart skipped a beat. He looked so natural on horseback, his posture balanced and effortless as he led Moody down the narrow dirt path. It was easy to imagine him as a rodeo champion, his athletic frame graceful and controlled.

It wasn't rare to find herself staring at this strong, beautiful man, asking God what she'd done to deserve him. He'd been her refuge in the storm, and then, once the storm had passed, he'd been her new beginning.

Once her battle against Walters had ended, Isadora had been surprised at the void it left behind. For the past ten years, her single-minded focus had been justice. Once she'd achieved it, she'd felt relieved but strangely…lost.

The feeling hadn't lasted long. Dex, Oliver, and ranch life had offered her a purpose, a fresh start on life, and a heart full to the brim. For the first time since her mother's passing, she felt…

Home.

She patted Skinny's warm, sleek coat affectionately. Yeah, country life suited her just fine.

The narrow, wooded trail opened to the sunlit glen, dotted with purple and yellow wildflowers, and…and…

A foundation for what looked like a new cabin? Here, in the middle of her favorite spot on earth?

She jerked her head to Dex, who was watching her reaction, his eyes alight with anticipation.

"What…?" Her mind raced, along with her heart. "What's this?"

"Something Oliver and I have been working on."

Isadora's lips parted in surprise, and she melted. A cabin, just like Dex had built with his dad when he'd been Oliver's age.

Dex climbed down from Moody, then came closer to help her dismount. He wrapped his hands around her waist and slid her to the ground, facing him.

"It's the foundation for a cabin we're building. For all of us."

Giddy excitement shimmered through her. *For all of us.* "To replace the cabin that burned down?"

Losing the cabin he'd built with his dad had been an emotional blow. It had been his refuge since he was a boy.

Dex's expression softened, and he took her by the hand. "It won't be like the old one." He looked deeply into her eyes, tracing circles over her palm with his thumb. "Sometimes, life gives you a chance to start something new. First, you need a foundation. We've built that, Isadora. Together."

Her heart raced, because she realized he wasn't just talking about this cabin. He was talking about *them* and their life together.

"We've built our foundation on trust. Love. And the certainty that we will be there for each other, no matter what. This foundation is strong enough to build the rest of our life on. It can weather any storm."

Tears welled in her eyes. He'd proven time and again that he would stand beside her, love her, and keep her safe, no matter the cost. It was a promise as solid as the ground they stood on. She'd never felt as sure of anything in her life.

He pulled her closer and pressed his forehead to hers, squeezing his eyes shut. "Isadora de la Cruz, I am madly in love with you. I have been since the moment you sauntered up to my ranch with those big, vulnerable eyes and tough-guy attitude."

She laughed, even as a sob bubbled up in her throat. This man made her feel so much, all at once.

"You've faced fear and heartbreak, yet you're so strong. The fire and courage in your spirit has pushed you forward through the darkest moments. I never want you to have to face those dark moments alone again." He pulled back and swept his intense blue gaze over her face, the raw emotion in his eyes stealing her breath. "Isadora, I brought you here today to ask you..." He sank to one knee and pulled a small velvet box from his pocket.

Her heart hammered against her ribs, and warm tears poured down her cheeks.

"...if you would grant me the honor of spending the rest of my life with the bravest, strongest, most beautiful woman God has ever made. And I promise, with every piece of my heart, to love, cherish, and protect you for all of eternity." His handsome features shone with a love so fierce it reverberated through every cell in her body.

"Isadora." His voice was rough and thick with emotion. "Will you marry me?"

"Yes," she whispered, her throat choked with tears. "With all my heart, yes."

He leapt up, gathered her into his arms, and whirled her around. She threw her arms around his neck and half laughed, half cried, her cheek pressed to his.

Slowly, he lowered her to her feet, his eyes never leaving hers. "You have made me the happiest man on earth." He opened the little box and waited, holding his breath.

She caught sight of the stunning diamond atop a golden band and gasped. "Dex, it's…oh my word…it's the most beautiful ring I've ever seen."

His breath rushed out of him. "May I?"

She pressed her lips together, tears stealing her voice, and nodded.

He took her hand and slipped the ring onto her finger, his warm, callused skin rasping over hers, his eyes studying her nervously. "You're sure you like it?"

"Like it? That's the understatement of the century!" She angled the stone to see it twinkle in the sunlight.

He chuckled, then drew her close and kissed her long and slow, her salty tears sliding over their lips.

She threaded her fingers through his hair. "I can't wait to tell Oliver."

"And my parents. They're already in love with you." His words were a murmur as he brushed his lips over the curve of her jaw.

Isadora hadn't known it was possible to feel this happy. Euphoria rushed through her veins, lighting her up from the inside like a Christmas tree.

He gathered the reins of both their horses, then lifted her

onto Moody and climbed up behind her. "Ready to go share the good news?"

She turned and gazed into those incredible blue eyes that made her heart stutter *every time.* "I love you, Dex. And I am *so* ready to share this news!"

He pulled her close and pressed a lingering kiss to her lips. "And I am so ready to share the rest of my life with you, Isadora de la Cruz."

* * * * *

Fall in love with stories where faith helps guide you through life's challenges, and discover the promise of a new beginning.

Look for six new releases every month, available wherever Love Inspired Suspense books and ebooks are sold.

Find more great reads at www.LoveInspired.com.

Dear Reader,

Thank you for coming along on this adventure with Ruby and Dex! I loved escaping to the ruggedly beautiful Montana mountains with a mysterious heroine and complex cowboy as my guides. I can't resist Western settings under the big sky and thrilling stories unfolding in all that wide, open beauty.

Ruby's strength and fiery spirit are admirable, but her painful past and need for connection lend her a vulnerability that so many of us experience. Dex's past has also left its scars, and his journey toward trusting again falls in step with the path many of us walk every day. Fortunately, they have the Lord on their side, guiding their way to healing and love, just as we all do.

If you enjoyed Ruby and Dex's story, please reach out and let me know! You can find me on Facebook, Instagram, X, and Goodreads, or visit my website, JulieArnoldBooks.com.

Warm regards,
Julie Arnold